My first book is dedicated to my beautiful wife Jessica.

Thank you for always standing by my side and

believing in me. Your encouragement through the

tough times and selfless desire to see me happy are

what made this possible. Well, that and my parents.

Mom and Dad, you have been a blessing. Thank you

for being so great and understanding, but I gotta give

this one to Jess. She suffered though the hardships and

my terrible temper. Furthermore, If I didn't mention

you... Its for a reason. .... JK........

Ghost Station

Motionless sitting back in his chair he appears at rest but his mind races. The captain tries to imagine how these once lowly outlaws found a way to pay for the huge shipment of weapons he is bringing them. With the information he has, he just can't think of a logical explanation, but he cannot ignore what a payday like this could mean for his bottom line.

Knowing he must change his focus, he begins to come up with ideas for many possible scenarios. If he is heading into a setup contingencies will trigger his actions, and he plans on being prepared for them. He even comes up with ideas for events after the initial contingencies. He plans so much the idea of a strait forward payment-for-product deal becomes almost disappointing, but luckily there is someone more rational to assist him.

"Sam, it's time to get ready. Let's check your equipment," a female voice tells him.

Sam opens his eyes and looks at the woman standing next to him.

"Alright. Thank you for bringing me back to reality. Some of the ideas going through my mind were pretty far out there," Sam tells her.

"Don't tell me it got to the point of open airlocks again."

"Yes. It always does," he says with a grin.

"Someday I'll understand your fascination with launching things out of airlocks," the woman tells Sam.

The woman standing next to Sam is much more than she appears to be. Named Roczi, she is an artificial intelligence from the Machine home world, Venus. Venusian A.I.'s are expected to interact with Humans for no less than 5 years in some type of employment. This period is called an Observance. It is similar to an internship, but it's purpose is only to observe human behavior. Whatever the reason for this requirement, it has brought Sam an excellent personal assistant, for next to nothing, over the last 2 years.

With her adjusting body, Roczi can look however she wants, as long as it's in the parameters of her telescoping frame. Currently she's a short brunette with bob style hair. Although young for an A.I. she is remarkably Human like, and has been since before meeting Sam. To Sam's dismay, Roczi is nearing the end of her Observance and could choose to do anything she wants afterward.

Working with Sam she has spent most of her time without Human contact, except for conversations with Sam and the brief passing of instruction from docking bay staff at different places they have gone. Sam has introduced her mostly to smugglers, illegal arms dealers and other criminal types. Needless to say, Sam has not been a good representative of Human behavior or social norms. Luckily, Roczi assures Sam her previous Observance time was spent at fine society hotels, restaurants, and auditoriums.

Sam on the other hand, is pretty well known throughout the Venusian government for his role as a Human diplomat to Venus during it's development period. What the Machines must never know, is what he was actually doing there. Unfortunately for Sam, he was shelved by his commanders immediately afterward. Worried Sam's cover could be blown after the fact, administration put him behind a desk indefinitely. In response, Sam ended his service with the UNSA shortly after his operation on Venus ended. Although, Venus was the only theatre of operation Sam served, he did manage to develop agency contacts throughout the solar system.

Barely content with his new role in life, he sells his wears mostly to frontier settlements, but he also sells to the bandits that attack those settlements and the shipping lanes between them. The majority of his money is made from settlements gone wrong. Often different groups go to war, and often his former employer intervenes, but when they don't Sam brings his influence to the conflict. Afterward, Sam leaves without concern for the outcome.

"Sam! You really need to focus. This is not your normal merchandise sale. Criminals are purchasing the means to become full blown pirates, and quite frankly, neither of us believe they have the credits for this transaction," Roczi reminds Sam.

Sam then sits up and looks at the navigation control panel.

"You're right. Gotta get myself in the right mindset," is his groggy reply.

Sam then pushes himself out of his captains seat and takes a look at Roczi. He forces his eyes open a little wider, then walks to the back of the ship. When he arrives at the armory he places his hand over a reader and the door slides open. What lies inside are some of the most advanced weapons and equipment available. This includes thin fabric armor suits that work by dispersing and redirecting energy, and human enhancement suits. The enhancement suits work by stiffening and contracting in sync with human muscle and bone. The armory also holds a large array of weapons and guns. Magnetic, plasma, and energy weapons are all kept there, as is the always reliable firearm. Beyond the guns, E.M.P., fragmentation and plasma grenades are also kept there.

Sam puts on the suits, grabs a 10mm magnetic Trident pistol, and covers them all with a black, over sized, sensor filled coat. If a signal or environmental change is to occur, Sam and Roczi will know about it.

Sam conducts a series of tests after the enhancement suits are on to make sure the sensors are working properly. He then leaves the armory for the full body mirror in his quarters. There he goes over his overall appearance. He makes sure sensors and enhancements are hidden under his grey trousers, grey shirt and black coat. He also goes over his outward looking physique. Sam strives for a healthy, distinguished image, believing a softer more complacent look could lead others to believe he is soft and complacent. He goes over his short black hair and shadow of a beard. He checks his teeth for debris and whiteness. When no grey hair or flaws of any kind are found Sam looks into the mirror and confidently, somewhat arrogantly, decides he is ready.

Clearly at ease, Sam enters the bridge and walks up behind his captains chair and places his hands on the backrest. Then he focuses his eyes on the screen.

"The rest seems to have done you well Sam," Roczi tells him.

"It wasn't the rest."

Seeing their location on the screen, Sam decides it's time to set events in motion.

"We're getting close. Send out a shallow hail. Then we wait for a response."

Roczi does as requested. Then the two patiently wait. Several minutes pass before they receive the response they are waiting for. It comes in the form of a soft female voice through the ships communicator.

"This is the Gargoyle. Please identify yourself."

The voice coming through the communicator is so clear it could be a person on the bridge with them, and Sam looks at Roczi and gives her a subtle nod.

"Gargoyle, this is the November. We have been scheduled to dock with you at this location, at this approximate time. Permissions have been granted by your Captain Saunders. Please disengage your cloak and engage docking beacons," Roczi answers.

"Negative November. It's our policy to auto dock every vessel to avoid damage to either ship or station."

"Acknowledged Gargoyle, but it is our policy to never allow control of the November to be given to anyone other than Capt. Stix. This is not negotiable."

"Stand by November," the gargoyle controller requests.

Roczi looks over to Sam for guidance.

"Prepare to leave quickly. If they don't agree we need to go. Any sign of weapons Rox?" Sam asks.

"Negative Sam."

Then the voice comes back through the communicator.

"November, the Capt. has agreed. We will be disengaging the cloak and engaging the docking beacon."

"I copy Gargoyle," Roczi replies.

Well within viewing range of the November, a
space station begins to appear off the stern of the
ship. It's an older, medium sized, circular station
with two rings and three internal docking bays.
Luckily, the November is just small enough to fit
inside one of the station's internal bays. The
station also has a highly elliptical orbit around
the Sun. This is a preferred orbit for many trying
to stay hidden from authorities. Soon a white
beacon light begins to flash on the station marking
a designated docking bay.

"Here we go Rox. I'll be in the cargo hold.
Dock us and follow my instructions."

Sam then leaves the bridge and enters the
November's dimly lit cargo hold. There he takes
another look at what he's delivering. As he does it
only serves to broaden his belief that he is
walking into a trap. Sam then closes his eyes and
takes a breath. He hears the November dock in the
station's cargo hold, then turns around and faces
the bay's ramp. One final bang rings through the
hull of the November, and a moment of silence
passes, followed by a short period of thought.

"They can't afford this...," he quietly tells
himself, then he takes a moment before his next
order.

"Lower the ramp."

Roczi begins to slowly lower the bay ramp. As
the ramp lowers, the extent of Sam's merchandise
can be seen. There are many crates of small arms
and 2 gun pods, but as the ramp continues to open
the real meat of this deal is made clear. Six

combat droids, nearly 3 meters tall and 1.5 meters wide stand behind Sam. Gun metal gray, armored, heavily armed, and capable of space combat these machines are almost unstoppable.

Sam walks down the ramp and finds Captain Saunders waiting in the Gargoyle's bay. A menacing site himself standing about two meters tall with a long gray beard and shaved head, but his mechanical left arm puts his intimidation factor just a little over the top.

Saunders' attacks on shipping lanes have increased, and he appears ready for larger targets, but his raids are still entirely pulled off by family. Still, Sam and Roczi are finding it difficult to believe they've acquired enough funds to make this purchase.

Captain Saunders can now be seen near the bottom of the ramp, and Sam notices his eyes widen with excitement as his expected delivery becomes reality.

"Sam Stix! I'm so happy to see you partner! I have to talk to you about the future." Saunders tells Sam in an excited tone.

"With the equipment you're buying there must be an exciting future ahead of you."

"Ha ha! Yes Sam. This may be the beginning of an empire. Come with me to the conference room. You'll get your money. Then we can talk about what's coming."

Sam agrees and walks with Saunders through his docking bay, but Sam still doesn't trust the bandit. The whole time Saunders is talking about some new trade route between the inner planets and the moons of Saturn, but Sam only catches bits and pieces. He's to busy watching for signs of hostility and keeping his distance from his synthetic arm. As the two walk out of the bay and into the corridors of the station Sam's situational awareness is in the red, and shortly after the door closes behind him his concerns are confirmed.

"Weapons signatures charging 50 meters ahead of you," Roczi calmly tells Sam over his earpiece.

Angered but prepared, Sam instantly grabs a dagger from under his coat and performs a 180 degree spin, thrusting the knife into Saunders upper back. The blade settles just below the neck, severing his spine. It happened so quickly the bandit doesn't notice the blade till the tip exited out the top his chest, but sam's dagger is more then a knife. Automatically the blade's sensors feel the insertion into flesh and inject oxygen and phosphorus into the victim, incinerating a large area of the back, neck, and chest. Sam then completes his 360 spin hitting the blade handle with his left hand, separating the head from the ash and cinders under it.

"Two pursuers have entered the corridor and will engage in moments. Sam, one of them is a machine!" Roczi tells him with urgency.

Sam's expression quickly turns from the stone face of focused anger to the look of a man about to fight for his life, but luckily the advent of A.I. mercenaries was planned for.

"Roczi, E.T.A. on back up?"

"Approximately one minute if I can get the Gargoyle's doors open."

"I'll hold them until it arrives. If the doors can't be overridden conduct a physical breach. I'd rather take my chances against the vacuum than the machine," Sam tells her as he aims an E.M.P. grenade toward the incoming threats and launches it.

Sam rapidly reloads with a plasma grenade and sends it toward his attackers. He then slips behind a maintenance door to the side of the corridor. A split second later a sharp pop is heard and the corridor darkens, then a bright light and burst of heat come around the curvature of the corridor.

"Roczi, give me an update."

"The Human is of course neutralized, but the merc is only slowed. Probably switching to a firearm or resetting his energy weapon. Cargo doors are..."

At that moment a bright flash and a loud boom rings out. Just beyond Sam's cover a grenade had gone off. Momentarily stunned and confused, Sam collects himself quickly.

"Rox! Are you there? Roczi, do you copy?"

Roczi does not answer Sam's call. Instead a more menacing voice comes through his communicator.

"She does not. It's just you and me. My backup is coming, but you'll be dead before they arrive," the reverberating voice of a machine announces.

Sam is left with useless sensors cut off from Roczi's Intel, but he stays cool. Sam tosses frag grenade into the hallway then enters into a service corridor. He runs away from the machine as fast as his feet will take him, but the mercenary enters the corridor shortly after in pursuit. Even with the enhancement suit aiding Sam's running the A.I. chasing him is slowly closing the gap.

Sam soon reaches a part of the service corridor with a large amount of electrical wiring and runs through a door. There he finds himself in the station's kitchen. Sam finds an opportunity in this and quickly sets up a simple trap. By putting a refrigerator in front of the door and pinning his last fragmentation grenade between them, Sam has set up what would be a fatal trap for a human. How this trap will effect a machine is yet to be discovered. He then runs for cover behind a large prepping counter in the middle of the kitchen. Shortly thereafter the machine kicks the door open and tactically enters the room. Firing two shots at him, Sam distracts the machine from the grenade rolling on the floor behind him. The machine returns fire, but the grenade explodes and the mercenary's sent flying through the air to the other side of the kitchen. As soon as he hits the wall Sam starts shooting. The bullets hit their mark but they clearly don't do enough damage. The machine shoots back, and gets an indirect hit on Sam's back as he dives for cover to the other side of a prepping counter.

"You stupid animal! I was going to kill you quickly, but now I'm ripping you apart slowly," the machine exclaims.

Incapable of replying, Sam quick crawls out of the kitchen and into the main corridor. The body armor may have done it's job, but the high speed projectile still knocked the wind out of him. Gasping for air, Sam manages to stand and begins heading back to his ship. Fortunately, the machine's legs were damaged by the blast preventing him from his murderous pursuit. Sam may not be capable of killing the immobile machine, but at least he can now get away.

In the hallway Sam can hear his reinforcements charging throughout the station. Gunshots and pounding footsteps mark their arrival. A giant combat droid runs past Sam paying no attention to him. Then he sees Roczi strolling down the corridor with a big smile on her face as the two approach each other.

"I hope I wasn't to late Sam," she tells him.

"To late to save me, but I happen to be a hard target," he tells Roczi as the sound of gunshots ring-out in the background.

"You must have ran across the softest A.I. merc in the business. Tell me how you got away from him."

"Can't you just acknowledge the fine work I performed here?" Sam asks.

"That's not how our relationship works. Besides, I don't want you to think you can do this without me."

"I'll tell you how I got away later, first I want to get out of this gear. Set the droids to capture defense and search for survivors. I'll meet

you on this bridge after I've changed and thought
out our next move."

Sam walks back to his quarters on the
November holding his ribs and wincing, still
wheezing from the gunshot. About 40 minutes later
Sam arrives on the Gargoyles bridge. Stiff drink in
hand, He walks up next to Roczi and takes a long
thirsty drink and he asks for the report.

"There are seven dead no survivors, including
the A.I.. The man in the corridor near the docking
bay you killed with the grenade, Captain Saunders,
three on the bridge, the oldest son, the daughter
and the wife, and one more of his sons went out in
a hopeless fire fight further down the Corridor.
The Venusian in the stations kitchen, he was a
known mercenary named W-385. He was better known as
Webs. The station has some internal damage, but all
major functions and hull integrity are fine. As an
added point of interest, this station is not on any
charts and thanks to us, it appears to be
uninhabited."

"It's a ghost station," Sam says quietly.
"Yes."

Sam quickly realizes he has stumbled upon a
wonderful opportunity, and nearly as quickly begins
taking advantage of it.

"Hack the Computers and take control of this
station. Find a way to clean out the Saunders
account. I delivered the equipment and I will be
compensated."

"I'm on it," Roczi replies as she turns to
one of the bridge control panels.

"I only hope they have the credits in their account to pay for my extra services. I had no idea I'd be performing six funerals today."

"Seven Sam. Remember Webs?"

"Of course Rox. He should have a bank account, so clean it out too. Leave the equipment here. No need to sneak it by customs if we don't have to."

"That's not what I meant, but I got it. Is there anything else?"

"Yes. Change the stations orbit, and it's name. Gargoyle is a ridiculous name for a space station. Um, something that commemorates this battle, and my victory," Sam tells Roczi with a smile.

"Fine. I christen this vessel the "Escape". To commemorate your heroic fleeing from a superior enemy."

Sam faces Roczi and gives her a disapproving look.

"A little less honesty would be appreciated."

The Job

Arriving at the customs space port from his newly acquired space station was routine and uneventful. Still, Sam was tired and decides to get a room on the giant customs station orbiting Earth. From the port all spacecraft are put through some type of search, and all are thoroughly disinfected with chemicals and intense heat before they can enter Earth's atmosphere. Most people just avoid the hassle and time involved in taking a ship planet-side, so they pay the fee to dock at the station then shuttle to Earth. Sam, on the other hand, would rather to take the November back to his large property outside of Phoenix Arizona, but this is not going to be his usual stay.

"Sam, get up! Wake up Sam!" A woman says to Sam as he sleeps in his suite.

Disoriented, Sam does not immediately recognize the voice or understand his situation, but he starts talking anyway.

"You didn't mention anything about a boyfriend?" Sam says somewhat jokingly.

The room gently brightens, and he finds Roczi standing at the light controls.

"Something big is happening, and if we don't get out of here soon we may be stuck on this station longer than your patients allows."

"To tired to ask questions. Get the November out of quarantine and get us off of this station."   "We should start by running to the ship and flying out of here to anywhere as fast as we can. I'll send the station crew notification of our intent."

Sam, knowing better than to question Roczi, had already gotten out of bed and began to dress by the time Roczi finished her statement. Almost as abruptly as she entered Sam's suite, Roczi begins leading them through the station toward the ship. The brisk walk to the November is uneventful. The only time a customs agent even speaks to them is when the quarantine security officer informed them that their ship is not to approach Earth, and that, "Any attempt to enter Earth's atmosphere will result in a vaporized vessel," Which Sam and Roczi already knew. Once onboard the the November they quickly exit the station with only moments to spare. Then the station shuts down completely, and no one can leave or dock.

"So, tell me what's so important you had to wake me and pull my ship out of quarantine," Sam asks as they distance themselves from the space station.

"There was a single ship of unknown origin passing one of our science vessels. The information I have suggests that it may be an alien ship."

"First contact? Was the science vessel Human or A.I.? What information do you have on this?"

"The science vessel was A.I., and Human authorities were notified just after A.I. authorities. I informed you as I received the information and the customs station is now locked down as customs protocol dictates. A.I. communications are substantially faster than Human. Just one more reason it pays to have a Venusian on your team."

"Just the info I don't know please. You know, that wasn't very machine like," Sam interjects.

"Are you saying I'm Human like?" Roczi asks with a smile on her face.

"Not like a machine, but not Human either. It was more like an ass," Sam says back with a smirk.

A few hours into their space drift Sam's communicator begins to signal from his coat pocket. He pulls it out, but when he see's who it is, he hesitates to answer.

"What is it?" asks Roczi.

"It's my old boss, Zac... I need to take this in private," Sam tells her.

Roczi simply nods and heads back to her quarters. Once the door to the bridge closes Sam finally answers.

"This is Sam."

"Sam, this is Zac Van Tellure. We need to talk," He hears over the communicator.

"Would this be about the first contact?"

"What else could it possibly be about?"

The call was short and to the point, but the excitement Sam feels during the conversation could be seen in his pacing and gestures throughout the call. Immediately afterward, Sam walks to Roczi's quarters hoping to share what he had just learned. He swiftly strides through the November's shadowy, but clean and orderly passageways till he finds Roczi just outside her quarters waiting for him.

"This is big," Sam exclaims as he nears her.

"The ship your science vessel observed was an extraterrestrial species, and these aliens have made contact with our top military governments and the United Nations Space Agency. Van Tellure says they need me, and if I'm right and Earth politics hasn't changed, we could both be a part of it."

"I don't think Earth's leadership would allow a Venusian A.I. To be a part of this?"

"Don't count yourself out. I'm already thinking of a loophole to squeeze you through. In fact! I've already got one."

"Already found a way to blur and complicate opportunities from an old friend... I'm working for a fiend."

Sam simply ignores Roczi's comment and continues to explain his 'grey area' idea.

"The politicians haven't yet agreed on Venusian A.I.s being a form of life. Till then, I don't have to mention you at all. I can consider you equipment," he tells her.

Seeing the displeased look on Roczi's face, he quickly realizes his mistake.

"Please, don't call me equipment again," Roczi tells Sam in a scolding tone.

"That's not what I meant Rox."

Roczi simply raises an eyebrow as she looks at Sam with a crooked smile.

"I know. It's just fun seeing you squirm," she tells him.

Several hours later, UNSA space fighters are escorting the November to a small landing pad in the U.K., by passing nearly all customs policies. Once there, Sam is directed to stay in the ship until told otherwise. Soldiers then begin hosing the November down with acids and disinfecting it with flame throwers before Sam can exit the space craft, and when he does finally exit the ship there is a UNSA agent there waiting for him.

"Sam Stix, I'm agent Fletcher. Come with me and someone will brief you on... whatever it is you're here for."

"Thank you Fletcher. I'm looking forward to finding-out myself ."

Fletcher asks Sam to enter a military vehicle and come with him to the ruins of a castle a few kilometers away. Sam quickly agrees.

On the way Sam asks Fletcher a couple questions, but the agent claims not to have answers for him. Instead, Fletcher redirects Sam's questions back toward him. In turn, Fletcher's questions also go mostly unanswered, but in a way that sounds complete. Like two politicians working under corporate influence, nothing useful is accomplished. The conversation between the agent and former agent would be considered annoying to most people, but the two men are amused by the obvious nondisclosures.

They soon arrive at their destination and approach it's tall stone walls. They enter the castle through a simple small wooden door on the exterior wall. Beyond the walls is a small courtyard and another stone structure with several doors, but the door they approach has a large, rusty old padlock on it. Fletcher puts his fingers on the bottom of padlock and the door swings inward, but it only opens up to an empty room with a cobblestone floor. Fletcher enters the room with Sam just behind him. The door closes, and shortly thereafter an elevator comes upward out of the cobblestone floor. This brings a little smirk to sam's face.

"This really isn't what I expected. I've been out of the mix for years, but this is literally some 1960's spy stuff. Have there been budget cuts?" Sam asks cynically, but Fletcher doesn't appear amused.

"No. This is actually very effective. We tried holographic camouflage of structures for several years, but it turned out to be more of a marker than a cover. We returned to basics. It's just as convincing, but more cost effective. In fact, several criminal hideouts have been noticed and identified by their holographic camo, but I'm sure you'll be briefed on that. If not, consider this a heads up."

"Thank you, and I'm sure I'll be briefed on current developments," Sam replies.

Fletcher then goes on to tell Sam not to touch the walls of the narrow corridors he's going to enter shortly, saying his life could depend on it. Sam takes a look at Fletcher hoping to see a grin, but finds no smile to indicate he was joking. Sam then enters the elevator, and it quickly takes him down hundreds of feet. When the elevator suddenly reaches it's destination the door slides open to a long dimly lit hallway. Sam recognizes the purpose of the long hallway almost immediately. It is sometimes called "a late walk". Intruders or stumblers may get this far into the building, but they won't make it down the corridor. It is another effective measure in keeping the purpose of this structure secret.

Sam carefully walks down the stone corridor about 40 meters. Then the hallway opens up into a large three story, circular room with other long hallways leading into it. Nothing is marked, but shortly after Sam arrives at the room a green light appears above the corridor up and to the left of him. Red light is emitted from the other corridors. Sam manages to figure out which one to enter.

As Sam takes the stairway and enters the corridor it slowly leads him to yet another unmarked room. Carefully Sam walks through the door, just to find himself disappointed in another small square room. The door behind him slams shut and the holographic wall directly in front of him begins to disappear. All of the sudden, Sam finds a well dressed man standing just beyond the vanishing wall, and his feeling of disappointment turns.

"There's the hologram. I knew you had to have at least one," Sam tells Zac.

"How have you been Sam? It's truly good to see you."

"I'm good, and it is good to see you. I'd ask how you're doing but I imagine you are up to your eyeballs in work."

"Yes I am, and that's why we need to talk."

As Sam's agency contact and supervisor back when he worked for the UNSA, the two had once worked closely together. Unfortunately for them both, the UNSA still had not (and has not) publicly acknowledged that they have an Intelligence division. Because of this, Zac's official title is senior operations director.

seeing him for the first time in years, Zac looks just as Sam remembered, with salt-n-pepper hair, a perfectly groomed beard, and ocular implants in his brown eyes. Well dressed and slightly taller than Sam, he appears very conventional in his blue suit (with the exception of his ocular implants).

The two men begin walking through the large room with high gloss floors, walls and ceilings. They walk till they reach a large alloy table with a glass-like screen top. There Zac asks Sam to have a seat, and he begins his briefing.

"This is the information we have so far. An alien species made contact with us at approximately 0600 hours. They are requesting our help in a war they are loosing. To what extent is unclear, but they believe our military build-up can turn the tide and save their species, possibly even their home world. We have already agreed to allow refugees into our system, and have offered any of the solar systems planets or moons for terraforming and colonization, with certain obvious exemptions. There is also some stipulation about over colonizing."

"I hope your not asking me to watch their numbers Zac. Bean counting isn't what I do."

"No. No. The politicians are working out the details on that, and please let me finish. In return for our concessions they have offered science advancements. These advances are amazing and include the eradication of virtually all disease. There biosciences are so advanced that their scientists believe a person can keep their youth till the time they pass, at the age of three-hundred plus years. It goes without saying, that is huge for us, but they want their world back as well."

"What else are they offering, and please tell me we're not actually entertaining the idea of going to war with an ally we don't know against an enemy of unknown power or intent? No one in there right mind would even consider going on an offensive."

"There are a few leaders who still feel forming an alliance with these aliens could better our odds against a machine uprising. And these aliens, who call themselves Mirancris, insist this uprising will happen. They are feeding on the fears of the paranoid."

Sam then shakes his head with a disapproving look on his face. If there is one thing Sam left the UNSA with, it is the belief that the Venusians have no desire to rise against Earth.

"So, what is it you want from me?" Sam asks.

"Alright Sam. Among the many incentives the Mirancris have offered if we aid them in retaking their home world, there are some we want regardless. Those are near light speed travel, space warp tech, and their library of alien species and inhabited planets. This is the mission, and the reason you got the call. We have no idea how long they've been observing us, but I am guessing you were out before that time. Beyond that, you are still the only operative who consistently passed the A.I. deception tests. We have no idea what their capabilities are, but my hope is that if they have similar tests, you can beat them. The assignment is similar to the Venus-Pierce project you pulled off. Go in posing as a fact finding envoy to determine odds of victory if we assist. Get the information I mentioned or as much as you can. We want to know how they got here, what else is out there, and I don't plan on having to go to war for it."

"What happens afterward?" Sam asks.

"What do you mean?"

"To me Zac. What happens to me?"

"You stay in the employ of the UNSA."

"So I can be potted like a plant behind a desk somewhere, and threatened with treason prosecution. I have no intention of being placed back under the thumb of world governments. I can't come back Zac. I have no faith in the true intensions of the UNSA."

"Humanity needs you Sam."

"My faith in humanity is even weaker than it is with the UNSA," Sam says as he stands.

Then Sam turns away from Zac and begins to quickly walk out of the room.

"Wait! We can do this by contract. Two-million for the species and their planet locations, 3 for the N.L.S. Tech, and 5 million for the Warp tech. The mission is considered a failure without the warp tech, and all mission objectives need to be discussed in person, no coms."

"What about stipulations?" Sam asks.

"Simple, no disclosure of mission details or objectives. Nothing else. I need you on this Sam."

Sam pauses for just a moment, but it's long enough for him to bring his smile under control. It's a deal Sam can't ignore. Suddenly, the universe has flipped onto itself and a single person has an edge on the most powerful governments of Earth. To Sam and his tremendous Ego, letting this slip into someone else's hands is entirely unacceptable.

"Let's get me geared up. I'm going to take some personal gear as well"

"Whatever you need Sam, and thank you. I feel better knowing you're taking this one."

"I feel better knowing you reasoning behind it. The idea of going to war... I just can't imagine."

Tickets

Please

As he is driven to his ship, Sam finds Roczi standing by the November. He watches as the amber sky around her slowly sets behind a grass covered hill top. Soon, a military vehicle is also seen approaching the hill. It pulls up next to the November and a large man in a black tactical uniform gets out. Then Sam's vehicle pulls up to the November and he exits and walks up to the soldier.

"Is their something I can help you with," Sam asks.

"Yes. You can tell me where to put my bags and equipment."

"Did Van Tellure forget to mention something to me?"

"I'm guessing he didn't forget. He must have omitted this for his own reasons. I'm Lieutenant Nico. I'm here for your security, and the security of the mission. You must have known they couldn't have a contractor run this mission without agency eyes on it."

"Would I be wasting my time if I said your assistance is not necessary?" Sam asks expecting to be disappointed by the answer.

"Yes you would be."

Sam receives the answer he felt was coming, but he knows nothing will change Nico's involvement in the mission. He looks at Roczi and motions for her to help with the bags of equipment and crates. After Roczi and Nico bring the stuff onboard the November Sam takes the ship into orbit. He looks at the new member of his crew, and with an awkward grin on his face gives him a directive.

"Show me what you got."

Nico smiles and opens one of the large crates. Then he starts explaining its contents.

"First we have your armor and enhancement suits. The great thing about these suits are they have all been fully consolidated into one."

"Really! how did they manage that?" Sam asks.

"Don't know how they did it, but I can tell you from personal experience they work great. They are lighter, thinner, and more effective than the two previous suits."

"Can the suits be wired for third party situational scanning?" Roczi inquires.

"Yes they can, but these need the sensors attached. Upper brass never informed me of a third person being present on this mission, so I never had them equipped," Nico says as he looks at Sam with disapproval.

"Roczi is actually an A.I., and since no agency or government has confirmed A.I.'s as a life-form, she is considered equipment. I was granted any equipment necessary."

A short silence follows Sam's statement, till Sam speaks again.

"Roczi, would you take the suit and add the sensors please? What else do you have here Nico?"

Roczi extends her hands to Nico and he places the suits in her hands. Then he continues to explain the equipment he brought for the mission.

"Apparently, the Mirancris have put very few stipulations on having us onboard their ship, cause I've been issued several weapons, each in pairs. We got two compact triad magnetic assault rifles, two high energy light rifles, a pair of submachine guns, and sidearms. I assume they are for crew and

31

not equipment," Nico tells Sam as he pulls them out of a crate.

"Of course. The idea of gun wielding devices is absurd. Except for the fact there are hundreds, if not thousands, of them out their making a killing with them," Sam says cynically.

"The last piece is probably the most important. It's a tiny earpiece developed by the Mirancris and modified for Humans. It auto-interprets their language and the language of all known species. It also incorporates a small camera that can be placed anywhere for visual communications. I haven't met any yet, but I've been told some species communicate through visual means."

Sam is impressed by the equipment Nico's brought onboard, but he still looks at the physically intimidating lieutenant and wonders about his role onboard the November. Sam would hate to have a confrontational relationship with him for the duration of this mission, so he decides to get to know him a little better. Sam asks Nico about his time in the UNSA and military service. The lieutenant answers quickly.

"Well Stix, I've been an operator with the UNSA for nearly two years now. I was with Brazilian special forces before that. I would have stayed, but I wanted to get off world and hopefully see some action along the trade routes. The prospect of peace keeping on a settlement didn't bother me to much either. What can I say? I want to see action, but I couldn't say no to this. Serving on a contracted vessel in the early stages of first contact could possibly put me on a fast track within the UNSA."

"Glad to hear you're eager Nico."

"I can hardly wait to see one of these things up close."

Sam looks at the lieutenant and knows he's playing a bit of the innocent. No one gets into UNSA Intelligence with that kind of eager enthusiasm, or it's not the same agency he once worked for. Sam is inclined to believe the lieutenant is holding back. With his questions as answered as they will get, Sam heads back to his quarters for a little shut-eye, and when Nico says he would like to do same, Sam directs him to Roczi's quarters. It not like she uses it anyway. It's just one more advantage of being a machine. The two walk toward the back of the ship and Sam takes some of the equipment to the armory. Inside the armory, Roczi is tethering sensors to the suits. Sam walks up next to her and places a crate on the table.

"Does Nico have to be here? I'd prefer it to be just you and I," Roczi says with disappointment in her voice.

"Yes. He'll be here to keep an eye on us for the duration. He won't interfere. Besides, I'm sure he can be of service to us if things go wrong. I'm guessing he has elite combat training."

Roczi just gives Sam a little half smile and says good night to her as he leaves the armory. Exhausted, he heads back to his quarters and falls asleep when his head hits the pillow. Several hours later his alarm wakes him. Sam gets out of bed to find his new combat suit with his long black coat, grey trousers, and shirt hung up behind the door. As usual, Roczi has everything ready for him. Sam gets up, and suits up. He was nearly completely finished with his usual ensemble when he looks into the mirror and decides he doesn't look complete. Something is missing. Sam searches through his closet and finds a dark silver tie and matching tie chain. He puts on the tie and chain, then looks back into the mirror. Sam then gives himself an arrogant smile and walks out of his quarters.

As soon as Sam enters the bridge he sees Nico and Roczi. Nico is in the typical black suit of a dignitary's security officer, but Roczi stuns Sam in a beautiful backless burgundy gown. She looks classy and complete with matching gloves and a diamond necklace. Sam is so surprised by Roczi's dress that it nearly eclipses the giant alien craft on the bridge monitor.

"Wow Roczi. I expected you to wear a skirt suit or something similar, but you look wonderful."

"Thank you Sam,' she says with a smile.

"What brought this on Rox?"

"I may be the first A.I. the Mirancris encounter, and this is the impression I want to give."

"And what impression are you hoping for?" Sam asks.

"I'm going for a more "lovely to meet you" and less of a "let's work" feel."

Sam simply nods, then looks back at the screen.

"So when are we getting this show started?" Nico inquires.

"Right now. Roczi, make contact with the ship and get us docked. Lets meet our new friends."

Roczi turns to the November's communicator, and checks the monitor. She pauses for a moment as the ship slowly gets quiet.

The ship on the screen is twice the height of a hundred story building and unbelievably wide. One long, curved, dome shaped portion dominates the front, and two smaller domed sections lay side-by-side in the back. The bottom portion of the ship has what looks like a series of columns coming down in various sizes throughout it's entirety. It looks something like an inverted cityscape. The upper domes also have streaks of light coming from them, while the columns are speckled in light.

Seconds later, Roczi's voice breaks the silence.

"Mirancris vessel, this is the November. We are dignitaries from the UNSA approved by your ambassadors to come aboard. We are awaiting instructions."

A few moments pass before the response comes through. An odd sound of reverberating bass, knocks, and hums comes through the ship's communicator, but what comes through their tiny translators is very different. A female voice with a somewhat Eastern European accent is heard through the earpieces.

"November follow the beacon to the port side and dock. You will have to manually dock as we are currently unable to safely link our systems. Thank you and welcome to the Infinite."

The Short Mission

As the November approaches the the huge alien craft, beacon lights mark large bay doors on a column under the forward dome. They also notice tubes between the columns. The tubes connect the huge columns on the underside of the ship, and must be thousands of passages between them.

Strangely, with all the exciting new developments, one question is standing out in Sam's mind.

"Why did that alien have a Russian accent?" Sam asks out of nowhere.

"Why wouldn't they?" Roczi replies with a confused look.

"I just figured the translator would give her an American or English accent."

"Sam, what you consider a lack of an accent is an accent to those who you believe have an accent."

"Are you seriously forcing me to question your answer to my previous question?" Sam asks as he puts his hand on his chin and smiles.

"Let's just watch the screen Sam."

Sam and Roczi abandon their discussion and face the screen. They watch as the November passes through a field keeping life supporting atmosphere within the alien docking bay, then they land in it's center.

"Any suggestions on how to make first impressions?" Sam asks.

"I'm merely support staff. You're the contract envoy. That's just strange in the first place," Is how Nico responds to Sam's question.

"A Human should decide on behalf of Humanity," Roczi says the two.

"You see, this is exactly why a contract envoy is necessary. Watch and learn."

Sam has Roczi conduct an atmosphere check, followed by an area scan. Results find only small variations in nitrogen levels and gravity. Four alien lifeforms are also scanned, but one is different. One of the aliens is not Mirancris.

   The November's ramp lowers. Then Sam, Rocs,
and Nico walk down to see their welcoming party
standing about 8 meters directly in front of them.
Standing side by side are four humanoid creatures.
The two on either end are obviously security staff.
They are standing just under 1.5 meters and ware
dark brown uniforms with what looks to be short
alien rifles, but they have substantially different
appearances. One is tan with dark green spots or
patches on the skin, while the other is dark grey
with bright white pinstripes. Still, they are both
clearly the same species. Each has large black eyes
and no visible mouth or nose, because these
features are small and located on the under side of
their head's. Smooth skin and a long swept back
scull are also traits of this species. The third
alien is much taller than the others, and a pale
whitish color. Well over two meters tall, thin and
boney with eight fingers on each hand. This
creature has a round, almost featureless head, with
the exception of what appears to be jaw bones in
the chin area and top back of its head. No other
facial features are immediately noticed. It's
movements also look feminine, and give it a female
appearance.

   Although the tall creature was the only
different species, another Mirancris really stands
out. Just to the left of her, in a long black coat
with a blood red collar is the alien known as
Suphran. This is clearly an entity with authority.
Very different from the two security personnel on
the ends, his skin is glossy black with a moving

red stripe. The stripe looks as if it could be an entirely different animal slithering within him. His large translucent eyes even seem to be small yellow serpents swimming inside smokey dark crystals.

Then the same sound that came out of the November's communicator before docking is heard, followed by an immediate medium toned, gravely voice.

"I am Suphran, lead strategist of combat operations, and this is my assistant Kiten," The alien says as he motions toward the tall pale species.

"Great to meet you. I am Sam Stix, and these are my assistants Roczi and Nico," He responds to the alien strategist.

"Your assistant Roczi is not Human Sam. She is synthetic. I am not alarmed, just surprised. Your leadership said nothing of bringing a synthetic onboard."

"I wouldn't do anything as important as this without Roczi. She is a wonderful asset to have, and I see your assistant is not what I expected either."

"Kiten is Laurine. They prove to be very adaptable, and she is greatly appreciated. Come with me. You'll be shown to your quarters and then we can start."

The two Mirancris security staff stay in the docking bay with the November as the large bay doors close and the strange field disappears. Everyone else follows Suphran to an elevator that takes them up to a higher level in the ship. While in the elevator, they talk about the ship they are in and some of it's capabilities briefly before they reach their desired level. Once there, the door opens to a large empty corridor. Suphran tells Sam and his party that Kiten will lead them to their quarters and that someone will bring them to the bridge after they have settled in.

"Is there a schedule we are to be on while we are here?" Sam asks.

Kiten looks at Sam and the others as different color patterns begin to appear and scroll down her face.

"Yes. After you have been shown your rooms and allowed time to settle, we will take you to the bridge. There you will meet the Captain as well as other ambassadors from Earth. A further description of this vessel and it's capabilities will be given. After all have arrived, you will be asked to report to a conference room where your discussions will take place," Kiten explains with her scrolling facial patterns and colors.

Despite the Laurine's unique language characteristics, the translator conducts it's job perfectly.

"I wasn't expecting to meet another life form on this ship. I'm curious about you and your species," Sam tells Kiten as they walk through the ship's corridors.

"I am Laurine. We are from an aquatic planet with a secondary ecosystem in the treetops that cover most of the planet. My people are from those treetops. The damp living conditions and many predators have kept us from developing into a space faring species, but we have been expanding outside our planet and into new areas since meeting the Mirancris, and to a lesser extent, the Theon. You could say, their war has given us a chance for further advancement. Currently most off-world Laurine are mercenaries, or security with expanded duties. That's due to our ability to multitask so efficiently."

Roczi is intrigued to find-out individual Laurine are fighting for both opposing forces as mercenaries, and can't help but try to dig deeper into the matter.

"Their are Laurine fighting against the Mirancris as well?" Roczi asks as they near their rooms.

"I'll let Suphran brief you. Here are your quarters. Get yourselves situated then you will be shown to the bridge."

The three thank Kiten and enter their large suites. Each suite is furnished very well and fully automated for the comfort of dignitaries. Kiten exits the area, leaving the three to themselves.

Roczi sets her equipment down in her room and leaves almost immediately. She brings some small electronic bands to Sam in his quarters and tells him to put it on as she hands it to him.

"What is it?" Sam asks.

"It's a location and body monitoring device. It will give me your location, and an idea of your situation."

"Will you be setting up Nico with one."

"Yes. That is, if he allows it."

"Good. I think I'll be utilizing him more than expected. Would you summon him please."

Roczi sends Nico the message, and a minute later he enters the room. Sam gives Niko the device and explains what he and Roczi had already discussed. Nico nods and pulls out his communicator so Roczi can check the link. It works perfectly, so Sam sends his requests to Nico, as not to say them out loud. Nico reads Sam's request and again nods in agreement.

"Let's take the bridge tour," Nico states, obviously happy with his advanced role in the mission.

The three exit Sam's quarters and find a Mirancris soldier waiting to for them in the corridor. He advises Sam and his team that he will lead them to the bridge, and Sam quickly agrees.

The walk to the bridge is a long quite one. The corridors look marbled and have very high ceilings for such a short species. Occasionally they pass alien writings and signs, and Roczi is putting them together as they walk by. She processes the symbols and learns more about the Mirancris language with every word they pass.

The three reach their destination and find other envoys and their staff already on the bridge. The envoys are conversing with the Mirancris bridge officers, so Sam starts looking around for someone to get information from. He soon spots what appears to be a group of officers, and focus on singling out the influential. Eventually, the Executive Officer and Captain are picked out of the group.

After a quick look at the Captain, Sam decides to engage with the Executive Officer, since the Captain sounds as if he is discussing himself and his career more so than the ship. Sam leads his team to the X.O., who was already discussing the different speeds the ship can travel and the purpose of the vessel. The X.O. is wearing a crimson uniform with a black collar and cuffs, and like the captain, his appearance is also different from every other Mirancris. This gives Sam the impression that everyone of the species may have a different skin pattern.

"Does the ship travel through warp locations or can it some how jump to different systems?" Sam asks the X.O..

"In the past we used wormholes or warping outposts to travel, but the Infinite, as all modern vessels, actually folds space to it's chosen destination," The Executive Officer informs Sam.

Moments later, Suphran enters the bridge and silences the crowd for an announcement.

"Thank you for the tour Captain, but could I please have all of our guests join me in the conference room?" Suphran asks.

The Human envoys begin to follow Suphran to the conference room, and Sam gives Nico a look. Everyone leaves the bridge and Roczi steps a little closer to Sam, but Nico, not so subtlety, leaves the group.

"You think something may be happening," Roczi asks Sam.

"I have this feeling. I need to kill it or confirm it. Besides, Nico wouldn't want to just stand there in the conference room. He's thinking the same thing I am."

Arriving at the conference room, they see it resembles a round amphitheater with all the seats facing a glass platform in the center. Sam quickly recognizes the set up as a holographic war room. Everyone takes their seats around the transparent platform as Suphran and another Mirancris in similar clothing stand by. Once everyone is seated, they begin to speak.

"Thank you dignitaries from Earth for attending. I am Suphran and this is my associate Colonel Quasic. Our other counterpart, Commander Kaens, could not be here as we are still at war... and he tends to give the wrong impression," Suphran says with a slight laugh.

A hologram of a solar system appears over the glass platform, then Suphran continues. He explains that the system that has just appeared is his, and describes it as similar to ours but smaller. With a total of eleven planets and moons the system is already vastly inhabited for it's size. The Mirancris home planet is actually a binary planet system called Bigan and Nictwar. They are approximately 120,000,000 km from their sun, but lesser size and temperature of the star keep the planets in the green zone. Suphran also informs the crowed that both planets of the system are actually

46

very hospitable for Humans, with the exception of the extreme gravity of low tide, but high tide would be very comfortable.

Elsewhere in the corridors of the infinite Nico approaches their quarters. His first thought is to go directly to Sam's room, but then he remembers Suphran's initial reaction to seeing Roczi. Suphran was surprised and maybe even a little rude when he discovered she was a machine, so Nico passes Sam's quarters and opens the door to Roczi's. What he finds is Kiten standing right in front of him.

Without hesitation Kiten grabs Nico and pulls him into the room. At the same time Nico charges her, pushing the Laurine further in. The two separate and regain their balance inside the spacious living area, but Kiten remains closest to the door.

"You should shut that door. No need get anyone else involved," Nico tells his adversary.

Kiten lowers her head slightly and reaches for the door controls. The door closes and she locks it shut. Then her facial patterns begin scrolling.

"The accidents that happen when someone is unfamiliar with their surroundings," Comes through Nico's translator as she speaks.

Both share a brief moment and prepare
themselves. Each realizes it could be the last time
they communicate with another living creature, but
confident it wont.

The blade comes from the right, hooking toward
Nico's neck. It is followed by a quick overhand
strike in a sharp fluid combination. Nico avoids
her first strikes with a short duck and dives
backwards. Just as fluidly as Kiten's attack,
Nico's backwards dive rolls him onto his feet and
his blade is already in his hand.

Swiftly, Nico nearly places his blade in
Kiten's chest, but she anticipates the strike and
counters by grabbing his forearm. Going for the
quick kill, Kiten stabs at Nico, but her thrust is
quickly pushed away with the palm of his free hand.
Nico counters with a kick to her abdomen. His
strength enhancing suit aiding him, he knocks Kiten
against a wall. Nico quickly follows up with more
knife strikes and combinations. Not making the same
mistake, Kiten avoids these attacks with her own
series of parries and blocks. She uses quick single
attacks just to keep him at bay as she tries to
determine her next move.

Then Kiten dodges and counters a knife strike
with her own spinning backhand. Nico catches her
wrist and attempts to counter, but before he can
her featureless face rolls over the top of her
head, and the joints of her elbows reverse. Kiten
viciously punches Nico in the temple. Confused and

stunned Nico can only grab and hold her wrists as
he gets his bearing back, but the Laurine is not
out of surprises yet. Kiten's arms and legs quickly
separate, giving her Four more limbs.

Kiten wraps a pair of legs around Nico's
thighs and grabs his arms. Then she backs up
against the wall and quickly climbs up with her
other 4 limbs, taking Nico with her. Near the top
of the suite she turns upside down and hangs from a
small chandelier. By the time Nico figures out his
dire situation Kiten has already released the
chandelier and the two are falling to the floor.
Nico's head is the first to hit. Upon landing, the
cracking of the skull and snapping of the neck make
a dreadful sound, but Kiten enjoys the violence.

Pushing herself up, she looks over Nico's
motionless body. Kiten then puts her limbs back in
place and rips the sensor off his wrist. Kiten ends
Nico's mission and life early. Then she walks out
of the room to continue her's.

Meanwhile, well into Suphran's presentation
Roczi nudges Sam.

"Nico's heart rate is elevated, and adrenaline
is now present in his blood stream."

At the same time Suphran stops talking and
looks at a small monitor on the underside of his
wrist. Suphran then abruptly leaves the room,

handing the remainder of the presentation over to
Colonel Quasic.

Now Roczi looks at Sam with a shocked look.

"Sam, I'm not getting anything from Nico."

The

Unexpected

There is nothing strange about Suphran
entering the ship's bridge and walking up to the
Captain, but then he puts an alien version of a
shotgun up to his head.

"Captain, warp this ship back to our system,"
Suphran orders.

"I'm in command of this ship, and no one..."

Suphran pulls the trigger before the Captain
can finish. The shot knocks the captain back over a
meter, and flips his headless body. Suphran then
immediately faces the X.O. and turns his head into
a purple mist and flying chunks. Two of the
remaining three bridge officers jump out of their
seats and reach for their weapons as Suphran ducks
behind a control panel for cover. The two officers
pull their weapons, but Kiten enters the bridge
with two pistols at the ready. She kills one

officer, but the other finds cover. Unfortunately for him, Suphran is already there. Suphran intentionally shoots off his gun arm, then slowly walks up to him after he falls to the ground. He stands above the officer and points the gun to at him.

"Why are you doing this?" The one armed officer asks.

Suphran's answers this question by shooting off his other arm, leaving him screaming and bleeding to death. The only remaining bridge officer has his hands in the air, and had surrendered as the first shot was fired. Using the screams of the of the dying officer as motivation Suphran makes one single demand.

"Take us to synthetic space."

The officer quickly complies, entering the settings into a console in front of him. Suphran is pleased by his compliance. After all, he has no desire to kill his people, but no one will get in the way of his plans. The officer is rewarded by keeping his life, as the screams in the background slowly come to an end. Suphran then tells Kiten to have him turn on the boarding alert and abandon ship alarms. He also orders the locking of communications and control, and orders the officers memory erased. Suphran then tosses Kiten a small device that is supposed to administer a chemical to erase any memories within a short period of time.

Then the Laurine briefs the strategist on what she found.

"The human fought like a highly trained combatant, and there were devices in the machine synthetics room that envoys would not need. I find it hard to believe this group is what they say they are," Kiten tells Suphran about her search of Roczi's quarters.

"Then I was correct, as expected. Board their ship quietly. I want to find out who they truly are," Suphran Orders.

Suphran then leaves the bridge heading for the docking bay, and Kiten directs her attention to the bridge officer.

"You understood what he said. Is there a reason you're waiting for me to repeat it?" Kiten asks him.

Then the officer completes the tasks and within minutes the ship leaves Earth's solar system, quickly jumping to the warring alien system.

"It's done. May I go now?" The bridge officer asks in an unpleasant tone.

Kiten appears confused by the device Suphran tossed her, and the officer gives Kiten a typical Mirancris condescending look.

"You just put the device on my neck and press the button. It's not that difficult," He tells her with disdain in his voice.

Looking at the device she comes to understand it, but then she discards it.

"Thank you, but if you only understood your position as well as the device. I am Laurine, and I've lost interest in my directive ," She says to him, as she grabs his neck and puts the gun to his face.

The officer struggles to beg for his life, but Kiten is squeezing his neck to tightly. She waits only long enough to see the fear in his eyes before pulling the trigger.

Back at the conference room Sam and Roczi hear the automated alert.

"Boarders have taken the ship. All crew need to evacuate to the escape shuttles. This is not a drill," The alarm repeats approximately every 30 seconds.

At first all the Human envoys are confused, but they follow the example set by the fleeing Mirancris and everyone rapidly runs out of the conference room. Most of the Human dignitaries find themselves lost with their unfamiliarity with the ship. Luckily for Sam Roczi's memory will lead them directly to the bay housing the November, but they will see plenty of chaos on the way there. Mirancris soldiers run through the corridors, and Humans scramble trying to find their way back to their ships.

"Where is Niko," Sam asks Roczi in an urgent tone.

"I have no idea. He went dark shortly after he entered my quarters. Your suspicions must have been right," Roczi replies as they move through the chaotic halls.

"Is it possible he can be saved?" Sam asks Roczi as they enter the bay housing the November.

"I wouldn't leave him if I thought he were alive Sam."

Sam looks at the door then takes a short pause to think. In the meantime Roczi runs to the November to begin preparations. Moments later Sam hears Roczi over his communicator.

"Don't take long Sam. I'm sorry, but we both know he'll never be seen again."

Sam knows he's gone, but even though he just met Nico, the idea of leaving him behind weighs heavy on him. Common sense tells him there is nothing he can do, but hope keeps him waiting at the bay doors. Sam continuously attempts to reach

Nico by communicator, but to much time passes
without an answer.

"Sam it's time to go," Roczi tells him.

The warnings keep coming through the corridors
just outside of the docking bay till Sam and Roczi
can wait no longer.

Sam turns back inside the hanger and walks up
to the November's entrance ramp. Shortly there
after, the interior doors of the Infinite's docking
bay close and lock shut, and the huge exterior bay
doors open. Now, only an image distorting field
separates them from the cold vacuum of space. Sam
enters the ship and Roczi takes the November off
the bay floor for departure.

As the November leaves the Infinite they can
see unknown vessels approaching and attaching to
her. The discrepancies in what they are seeing and
what they have heard are noticed by both Sam and
Roczi.

"I thought we already had boarders?" Sam says
to Roczi curiously .

"That's what was announced over the loud
speakers."

"Get us away from this ship Roczi."

Roczi pauses to assess their new situation. Then a grave expression covers her face.

"Oh my God. Sam, I can't get us home."

"Why not? Where are we Roczi?" Sam says slowly as his expression changes to match hers.

Roczi takes a short moment to map out their location, and looks at Sam.

"We are over 38 thousand lightyears away from Earth."

Sam smiles and lets out an uncomfortable laugh.

"Maybe I should have brought more supplies," He chuckles as he sits, then leans back in his seat. Closing his eyes, he contemplates his new situation.

"You shouldn't be tired yet Sam, and I hope you're not planning to sleep on it."

"Course not. You know me Rox. I think better with my eyes closed... In a laid back reclined position with very dim light and silence," Sam says in a humorous tone.

"I think your situational awareness has been compromised. Do I need to relieve you of command?" Roczi asks partially joking, but partially serious.

"Mutiny would be a very negative point in your Observance. Have you learned enough Mirancris lingo to send a decent message?"

"Not decent but understandable."

Sam turns to his ships screen and views the escape pods evacuating the Infinite. He watches as the enemy vessels attach themselves to the giant capitol ship. Sam sits in silence for just a moment longer, deep in thought he comes up with a plan.

"Contact an alien vessel, not Mirancris their enemy. When you do make contact tell them that I am an envoy from Earth, and we seek assistance."

"I like the idea, but that may void our contract with the UNSA?" Roczi explains in a playful way.

Sam laughs, and shakes his head.

"I'm just trying to claw my way back to some place near Earth. I'd even settle for your pretentious Venusian Arts Cathedral if it would get us out of this mess," Sam tells her.

"We'll make it back Sam. If anyone can get us back home you can."

Roczi sends out a hail to all the ships in the area. No response was immediately received, but several long minutes later the November's sensors

pick up something huge coming around one of the
nearby moons. Roczi puts it on the screen.

As it slowly approaches it is clear that this
ship is not like the Infinite. The dramatic
differences between the Infinite and this incoming
vessel are distinct. The refined smooth surfaces
and elegance are not there, and the sparkle of
interior lighting exiting exterior windows is
missing. This thing is black as night. It's only
visible cause of the striped gas giant behind it,
and the light of this system's sun reflecting off
it's scarred metal plates. The plates are suspended
by fields around the ship. These monstrous plates
protect and hide the true shape and design of the
ship behind them.

This is a vessel ready for war, and it has
obviously seen it's share. The giant steel
gladiator continues to approach. Eventually the
ship stops and several of the metal plates distance
themselves further from each other. Beyond the
space between the plates, there appears to be large
bay doors opening. There are no beacon lights and
no instructions from the communicator, just an open
bay door.

"I'm guessing that's an invite," Roczi tells
Sam.

"Turn off all the lights and go in slow. I bet
we can be just as dramatic, and maybe even more
intimidating," Sam says smiling.

"There comes a point when inspiring your crew with confidence only makes a captain look delusional," She tells him.

Slowly, they make their way to the blackened ship. Entering the large docking bay, they find no field keeping in atmosphere and only a single dim light helping to guide the November in. The ship seems almost abandoned. The exterior doors close behind the November as it lands inside. Then a pair of double doors slide open off to the side of the bay. More dim light exposes a field keeping the life supporting atmosphere within the ships interior.

"Another invite? Rox, would you say that is an invite? Get my space walk gear out of the armory please."

Roczi quickly heads to the armory and returns with Sam's gear. Sam asks if he should bring a weapon, but then quickly thinks better of it. He puts his space walk suit on over his regular outfit and lowers the Novembers ramp. Walking down the ramp he now sees a silhouette has appeared In the doorway, and a very large one at that. The alien creature is humanoid, but substantially taller than an average person and over a meter wide at the shoulders, but half that at the waist. Strong looking legs and long powerful arms make the creature look similar a gorilla from a distance, but glare from the dim light proves it to have a smooth hairless body. It's obviously carrying a weapon of some kind but not in a menacing manor. As Sam and Roczi get closer they can see the alien is wearing body armor and has tan skin that seems to be blistered.

The two walk up close to the field and stop, and the alien takes a couple steps back into the light. This gives Sam and Roczi a better view of him. It's eyes are covered by some kind of protective lenses, but underneath the clear lenses are a pair of almost Human eyes. The only obvious difference between its eyes and a humans are the oversized green iris. It's head is shaped similar to a Mirancris' with it's swept back scull, but there is a very distinct jaw line and a large nearly lipless mouth.

Putting his hand forward the alien creature waves the two into the the interior of the ship. Sam and Roczi take a look at each other, then Sam walks past the field further into the vessel. Roczi immediately follows.

"The air is exactly like it was on the Infinite. Sam, they breath the same air as the Mirancris," Roczi tells him.

Sam takes his helmet off and takes a look around the ship. In the dim light he can see two more of the large alien species armed and armored walking toward them.

The alien again motions to Sam and Roczi.

"Come with me," He tells them.

The earpiece translator clearly works with this aliens language. Sam and Roczi follow the aliens through the halls of the cold dark ship. They try to speak with it, but it doesn't recognize their language. It's only answer is "Come with me."

Only after Sam and Roczi are escorted out of the bay does Kiten emerge from the November. She places a dormant device on the ship, and sees this turn of events as a wonderful opportunity.

Bring A Guest

As they walk down corridors leading to more of the unknown, Sam and Roczi must once again assess a new situation. They soon realize, although they can understand the new creatures the creatures can't understand them. At first Sam and Roczi consider using this as an advantage, but reconsider after taking in their options. Their best chance at getting home may be to talk their way there.

Speaking the Mirancris language as best she can, Roczi asks their new hosts for a way to sync their earpieces. One of the large new host species then takes out his earpiece and places it in his 4 fingered hand. He looks at Roczi, and she understands to place her's in his hand as well. The large alien touches the two earpieces and they begin to light up as they synchronize. Moments later Roczi takes Sam's earpiece and does the same. Then they continue their walk as the earpieces update themselves.

The hallways are dark and cold, and the walls are completely bare. Hard steel and composite corridors leave the echo's of footsteps unhindered as they quickly march to an unknown destination.

A large door comes into view as they approach a fork in the hallway. The door is unmarked and, other than it's size, unremarkable. Then it slides open to reveal a room even darker than the corridor they are in. They approach the doorway with their new hosts and their eyes slowly adjust to the dim light. By the time they enter the room Sam can make out a ships bridge, but Roczi never had issue with the lighting. More of the large alien species are manning control panels throughout the bridge, and one large thrown like chair sits in the center. The chair turns and the ships captain now faces Sam.

The bridge brightens slightly and the Captain stands. Even larger than the other crew onboard, Sam wonders if he didn't beat his way into command. Wearing a red and brown uniform he looks down at Sam and Roczi. Then the Captain takes a few steps down from his thrown like chair.

"I am Captain Threshing. Welcome to my ship, the Gate's End."

"Captain, this is my assistant Roczi, and I am Sam Stix. Thank you for your assistance."

"Sam Stix what are you doing here, and more curiously, what are you?" Threshing asks in a low toned voice as he steps closer to the pair.

"Roczi is a self aware machine from the planet Venus. I am Human, from Earth. I was put on a fact finding assignment to access the threat of extinction for the Mirancris and the possibility of brokering a peace between your two people."

"Just so you know Sam Stix, I don't like the fact that you arrived here on our enemies vessel, and as for the threat of Mirancris extinction..," Threshing says slowly and quietly as he looks up.

A moment passes before the massive captain repositions his gaze forward.

"If I was head of this uprising, extinction would be the only Mirancris option. Please allow me to ask you a question Sam Stix, Have your people thought of our interests? My people, by the way, are Theon," The Captain says to Sam.

"Is there someone I can speak with about the the interests of the Theon?"

"There is. I'll have my crew prepare to have you transported to the capital. There you can speak with our leaders, but at the moment I still have to coordinate this boarding."

The Captain then waves for another Theon to approach. The one who does is much thinner and slightly taller than Threshing, but still of the same smooth yet blistered skin.

"Lieutenant Rizac, please take our guests on a tour of whatever they want to see until the transport vessel is ready," Threshing orders.

"Whatever they want?" Rizac asks in a disapproving tone.

Threshing just nods. Then Rizac looks down at Sam and Roczi from his towering position.

"What would you like to see?" He asks.

Roczi and Sam look at each other then look back up at the Lieutenant.

"I've seen enough of the bridge. Do you have an observation area?" Roczi asks.

Rizac motions for them to follow as he turns toward another doorway. The lighting of the bridge returns to it's previous darkness as they walk toward the exit. Then the door opens to another cold, dark, steel corridor. As they enter the corridor Captain Threshing can be heard laughingly saying.

"Don't mind the lieutenant. He is... who he is."

Roczi looks back at the bridge as the door slides shut, catching a glimpse of the Captain in his chair. Rizac seems unaffected by the comment and continues to walk the few meters down the corridor to an elevator.

It's obvious the Lieutenant is not known for his charming personality, so giving him the task of escorting guests seems like a poor choice. Rizac makes the short, quiet walk to the observation deck elevators somewhat uncomfortable, and the featureless walls don't help. The elevator gives off a dim green light as it moves up, then slowly turns white as it gets closer to their destination. Then the lift stops, but the door does not immediately open.

"Either the view is terrible or your lift is..," Sam says with an audible laugh, but he is cut off by Rizac.

"Wait!" Rizac says in a clearly annoyed tone.

The elevator's ceiling disappears within the walls and the walls begin to slowly descend into the floor. The floor then reveals itself to be the outer hull of the ship and an invisible dome gives what would be an astonishing 360 degree view of the system, but the view is obstructed by the giant armor plates suspended hundreds of meters away.

"This was once a great observation area," Rizac says out of nowhere.

Sam and Roczi look at Rizac, then they look at each other. Roczi knows Sam well, and because of this she walks away from the two and focuses her eyes on what stars she can see.

"Then the war?" Sam asks.

"Yes. When I first arrived on this vessel it was called Divine Gate. She was a beautiful ship. She was my Heaven. Then her inner beauty was stripped for scrap and her exterior blackened for war. Reducing her energy signature left once bright, warm corridors cold and dark."

Then Rizac pauses for a moment and looks at the enormous steel plates surrounding the ship before he continues.

"When the sky was taken, their was nothing left to distract me. The last piece of my paradise was destroyed. Now I walk through a hell personalized for me. Disfigured and diseased with others like me, but I alone have seen what she was before. I don't know who I hate more for taking her from me," Rizac says with anger in his voice.

Sam is speechless. Trying to contemplate Rizac's words and references leave Sam stunned, and not having the words is a position Sam has rarely been in before. He searches for the question he wants to ask, and the proper way to say it, but he doesn't get the chance. Roczi returns before he can ask the lieutenant any questions.

"I've seen enough here. What else would you recommend," Roczi asks Rizac.

"I recommend taking you to the transport. I too have seen enough," Is Rizac's icy reply.

"Have you always been out here in space?" Sam asks the Lieutenant as they walk back to the docking bay.

"Yes. After my creation I was brought to the Divine Gate."

"Creation?" Sam says curiously.

"Yes. All Theon are genetic constructs. Originally we were designed for particular purposes, or in my case, places. Everything was wonderful until they began taking us off our original assignments. I was created for the Divine Gate, not the Gate's End."

Sam being Sam, immediately begins coming up with a way to exploit this hatred. It doesn't take him long to come up with an idea.

"I have a space station lieutenant. After this war you should come take a look at it. You may find a piece of your heaven there."

Rizac has no reply. In fact, he appears to tense and seems even more perturbed than he had previously. The silence continues for the remainder of the trip to the docking bay. Once they arrive at their destination Sam turns to the Theon.

"Contact me or I'll contact you after the war," Sam tells Rizac.

Sam extends his hand toward the Lieutenant, so the Lieutenant curiously extends his. Sam grabs his hand to shake, but Rizac pulls his hand away and steps back. The situation only gets worse when Rizac pulls out a side arm and points it at the two.

"Get off my ship, and take your tool set with you," He tells Sam.

Rizac then takes a step forward and shoves Sam into the docking bay. Now inside the bay, Sam regains his balance and stands strait only to find two armed Laurine and a Theon pointing weapons at him. In the adjacent corridor, Rizac doesn't give any orders to Roczi or even wait for her to walk in. He just holsters his sidearm and walks away. Roczi enters the bay in a calm, unthreatening manner, and the Theon officer puts his weapon away and pulls out what looks to be hand restraints. He then approaches the two.

"Turn around and give me your hands," He orders.

"We're prisoners? What have we done?" Sam asks as he complies.

"You confessed to negotiations with the enemy on board their vessel. You and your ship are being taken to the capitol."

"I said nothing of negotiations. I'm on a fact finding mission."

No reply comes from the Theon officer. He instead turns his attention to the Laurine mercenaries and directs them to bring the prisoners onboard. He then walks to the front of shuttle heading for the helm.

Suddenly Rizac enters the bay. The Laurine mercenaries see the Lieutenant, but the emergence of a Theon officer does not alarm them. Rizac's intentions remain unknown until his plasma blade shockingly beheads the first Laurine, and a sudden flurry of suppressed submachine gun fire tears the other apart. Both mercenaries now lay dead on the floor, but Rizac never pauses his advance to the shuttles bridge. He just tosses the plasma blade to floor in front of Roczi and continues.

Then the Gate's End's huge docking bay doors open, revealing the atmosphere retaining field. Roczi quickly turns her back to the blade and picks it up with her restrained hands. Roczi turns her head 90 degrees to her back, and uses this ability to cut the restraints off of Sam's hands. Sam then takes the blade and free's Roczi's hands. By this time the transport shuttle's bay ramp is down, revealing the November within. Rizac appears

71

walking outward from the shuttles cargo bay with a limp Theon officer over his shoulder.

"You were never going to be released, and I really want to see this space station of yours," Rizac tells them with a deadly serious look.

"We really need to hurry. Come with me," Rizac continues as he tosses the other Theon officer off the shuttle.

The three run to the shuttles bridge where Rizac pilots the transport out of the docking bay.

"How much time do we have?" Sam asks.

"We have no time. I need to get us to the other side of this moon to avoid the ships guns and interceptors."

"Roczi, do you know where we are?" Sam asks.

"Yes. Trying to explain where to go is the hard part."

"I need something. Captain Threshing has reassigned interceptors to our capture, and we have more trouble. A Mirancris space craft is hiding just outside the moons atmosphere," Rizac says in an urgent tone, but moments later the craft disappears from the screen.

"It warped or cloaked. Let's just hope it doesn't attack," Rizac tells the others.

"Rizac, warp us to this system before they capture or kill us!" Roczi says as she enters a location into the shuttles controls.

Rizac doesn't even look at the destination. He just pushes some kind of alien throttle forward. Then on the screen, space can be seen bending and twisting before them. Then the screen just blacks out, allowing the three a few minutes to catch their breath. When the screen comes back the image of a blue planet with a large vertical ring appears. It's Uranus, and knowing they are back in there home system brings relief and a smile to sam's face, but for Rizac, an unknown future lies ahead. Now the three look around the shuttles bridge and at each other. They wonder how this event will effect their lives.

We Want More

    With no immediate threats present, Sam, Roczi, and Rizac have time to reflect on the unexpected events that have brought them together. Although, still somewhat uneasy with his new guest, Sam brings the plasma blade back to Rizac.

    "What is this?" Sam asks about the blade.

    "That is called a Peijax. Thank you for bringing it. It would have been hard to part with," Rizac says as he extends his hand toward Sam.

    Sam places the device back in Rizac's hand and smirks as he remembers Rizac's reaction to his extended hand.

    "Looks like little more than a cutting tool," Roczi says with a smile.

"Because that's all it is," Rizac says to her, but he continues to describe the weapon.

"The Peijax was originally developed by Mirancris entertainment executives. It was used by my people to cut each others limbs off for the entertainment of wealthy Mirancris. It is now forbidden by the Mirancris, but that is cause we adopted the weapon as a symbol. Both of the fight we have within us and the cruelty of the Mirancris."

"Rizac, I have lots of questions, but I'm sure you have many of your own," Sam says to the Theon.

"I do. I really want to know about this station of yours. I'm sure it can't be worse than the Gate's End, but I want to know where I'll be spending the remainder of my shortened life."

"To be honest, I've only spent a very short period of time there. It's a smaller station, currently being protected by six combat droids."

Sam pauses for a moment to think about his last statement, then he looks over at Roczi.

"Please don't forget to set the droids before we get there," Sam tells her.

"You sure Sam? We may need them to adjust the Lieutenants attitude,"

Rizac interrupts with a laugh.

"I'm sure my demeanor will change as my situation improves. Please continue Sam," Rizac says to assure them.

Sam begins to describe the station. He talks about his confrontation with the Saunders and his battle with the A.I. mercenary. He's even honest about why he was there, and tells Rizac about the weapons, but he says very little about his UNSA contract.

Roczi informs sam that she's going to the back of the ship to check on the November, and Sam continues to tell Rizac a bit about the Human story and answers a few questions about our history. As it turns out the Mirancris and Humanity developed along similar paths. War, arms races, madmen and hero's are the early history of both cultures, but then there is a fork in the historical road. At a high point of technological advancements, Humans went moderate in genetic advancements but heavily into computer and machine technologies. On the other hand the Mirancris made substantial advances in computers, machines, and physics, but then their priorities changed. The Mirancris became intensely focused on biological engineering. The vast majority of advancements beyond that were computer tech for the sake of genetic advances. The Mirancris became obsessed with creating and altering life.

Rizac then goes on about Theon history. The short history of the Theon is intriguing yet predictable. The species was developed to serve and enjoy it, and they were perfectly happy in the roles we were created for. Even the Blood Blade Combatants loved their role. Actually, it's safe to say they loved their role more than most. It was retirement they dreaded. The combatants were called Gyvan, and their origin assignments were much more short lived than other Theon. Mounting wounds, newer classed Gyvan, and age slowly forced the older warriors out of the games. Once out of the positions they were created for they were given other assignments. Needless to say the new positions didn't satisfy their designed need for conflict and excitement. All Theon were eventually forced into different assignments, but the Gyvan eventually rebelled and others followed. When the Mirancris ordered other reassigned Theon to fight against the Gyvan or die, they to rebelled also. That is how their uprising began. The rebellion would have been crushed by the Mirancris' Theon security forces, but the Gyvan gladiators were able to dispatch them at a heavy cost. Nearly all Gyvan were killed in the early parts of the war.

All the talk about death gets Sam thinking about things Rizac had mentioned earlier, and he has to ask about his statements.

"Earlier, when we were talking, you mentioned Heaven. We have a belief on my planet of a single God that created the universe and everything in it.

Could this be the same faith we have on earth?" Sam asks.

"Their is a belief passed down from old Mirancris writings about God. From what we can tell, as the Mirancris developed their genetic advancements they slowly forced God out of their lives and took his place for themselves. That is one more of the mounting reasons we added to our rebellion. War in the name of God."

"Killing each other for God. We do that too."

"Truly? In our faith, killing is only for when we have no other option," Rizac tells Sam.

"You also said your life had been shortened. What did you mean by that?" Sam asks.

"The Gate's End is a perishing ship. Meaning the occupants are already dead. The Mirancris use an extensive number of biological warfare tactics. At some point a pathogen was released on the Gate's End. It's the cause of the blisters on the crew. The outbreak was not contained in time. All of us were infected."

"How contagious is it?" Sam asks.

"Don't worry Sam. The pathogen merely carries an enzyme that attacks our synthetic DNA. Only Theon are susceptible."

A moment later Roczi returns from the back of the ship, and Sam lets her know he's going to get some sleep. He then makes his way to the shuttles cargo bay, presumably to sleep in his own quarters on the November. Rizac simply leans back in his chair and follows suit.

While Sam and Rizac rest Roczi examines the Theon vessel. She looks for maps of other systems and locations of other life forms, but what she finds is a huge cache of information. Not only is their information about life in the galaxy, but tech, propulsion and science information. Roczi finds everything Sam was supposed to bring back to the UNSA plus extra. Nearly eight hours after Roczi began her search she is finished. All the information she found will be very valuable to the UNSA, and therefore very valuable to Sam. Roczi can hardly wait to tell Sam, so she doesn't. She enters Sam's quarters and wakes him.

"You get much sleep Sam?" Roczi asks.

"No. There's just to much going on at the moment. All the new developments unfolding, they leave the future completely unknown."

"We're not done with new developments either. I went through the ships computers and found a huge amount of information."

"What kind of information? Did you find what we need for the contract?"

"Propulsion and warp tech, inhabited planets and systems, and descriptions of all known intelligent life. They've all been found. There was also a lot of other info in the shuttles systems. Weapons, communications, and science information were also found."

Sam is ecstatic by this unexpected and tremendous news. So much so that he can't help but put his fist forward and shout "YES!" In celebration, but he collects himself quickly and turns his attention back to Roczi.

"Create a report and send it to me. That information should be very valuable," he tells her.

Then the two walk back to the bridge, were they find Rizac awake and spinning in the helmsmen's seat. Rizac spots the pair and puts his feet on the floor. His spin comes to an abrupt stop.

"My species doesn't sleep," Rizac tells them.

"That is interesting, but we're coming up on the station. I'll put it on screen," Sam tells him.

On the screen, the station appears off in the distance. Rizac steps toward the screen and watches as they approach. She's a dark and uninspired looking station. The three stay quiet as the station gets larger and larger on the screen. Then Rizac turns to Sam and Roczi.

"I'm not yet impressed. I feel as if I may have left my hell, but I may be walking into someone else's," Rizac says looking demoralized.

The quiet continues for a few moments, only to to be broken again by the Theon.

"Grant me a few requests and I will have the station ready for the highest ranking official," Rizac says in approval.

Sam and Roczi feel relief wash over them after Rizac's last statement.

The large Theon shuttle then uses an external dock near the center of the station, and they board the Escape.

Sam asks Roczi to take their new crew member on a tour of the station. Roczi quickly but reluctantly agrees. Sam then makes his way to the stations bridge to contact Zac Van Tellure on the stations main screen. Zac is clearly very surprised Sam managed to contact him, but he is also overjoyed.

"Sam! What's happening out there? We've lost contact with everyone onboard the Infinite," Zac tells Sam.

"Very significant complications is how I would label it. I don't know everything that happened, but the ship was taken by the Theon in the Bigan-

Nictwar system. Everything I do know will be in my report."

"Are our people safe?"

"I wish I could say yes, but I don't think so."

"We have already been questioning Mirancris leadership here, but they have no answers for us. Have you obtained any information? We may need it more than ever now."

"I have the information asked for, plus much extra."

"Excellent! What's the extra?" Zac says with relief.

"A lot of tech, weapons and science data. I plan on selling it to different companies."

"You're currently under contract with the UNSA. That information belongs to us," Zac reminds Sam.

"My contract was for specific information. Double my contract and I wont bother shopping it around," he tells Zac.

"We shouldn't be talking about this over the com. Some one could be listening."

"I got this info from a Theon shuttle after the Mirancris failed to keep us safe. Anyone listening will understand. Not accepting this info would be stupid. By the way, I made first contact with the Theon while I was out."

"Lovely," Zac tells Sam sarcastically. Then he continues.

"You got your contract as we agreed. I can't authorize another ten million for the previous contract, but I can offer you a second. I haven't cleared it yet, but I'll put my ass on the line for it," Zac tells Sam.

"What will this contract consist of?"

"It will be a general contract. Anything obtained will be reported to me and the UNSA."

"I'll be happy to be a part of it," Sam agrees.

"Get here and we'll go over the details. Speak with you soon," Van Tellure tells Sam. The he closes communications.

The screen goes blank and Sam summons his crew. Moments later Roczi and Rizac enter the bridge. Once they arrive Sam is happy to let his team know they have secured a second contract with the UNSA. It may have cost him millions in information, but it saved him possibly years in time and hundreds of thousands (if not millions) in court fees. The UNSA is highly unlikely to let contract details interfere with what they want. Roczi hears the news, and has a little something to say about this new contract.

"Wonderful! I hope it's just as dangerous and twice as weird as our last contract!" Roczi tells Sam sarcastically.

"Rox, lets get a list of items from Rizac. Just things he can use to make the the Escape more livable."

Rizac then turns and looks at Roczi. Clearly happy to hear Sam's directive, he walks up to her and advises her of a notable observation he has made.

"How fitting the name of your station is. It's like you knew when you named it," Rizac tells her.

"Yes, and I thought it was fitting even before Sam's last escape," Roczi replies.

Sam then let's Rizac know that he is in charge of the station while he and Roczi are gone. The Theon is stunned, but excited about the amount of trust and responsibility he has so quickly obtained, and he lets Sam know. In return Sam thanks Rizac for keeping him and Roczi out of some distant prison cell, but Sam continues to speak truthfully. He tell the Theon the only reason he's giving him such trust is cause he has no other choice.

Sam and Roczi begin walking to the exterior docking bay where the Theon shuttle is docked with the November still inside, but she has concerns that must be addressed.

"Sam, do you think it's wise to leave him on the station, alone."

"I think Rizac is truly what he says he is, besides we don't have the time to repair or maintain this station. When it comes to the Escape, Rizac is our best bet."

"Then what about maintaining Rizac?"

"What do you mean?"

"According to the data I grabbed from the shuttle, Rizac along with the entire crew of the Gate's End have been infected by a biological weapon."

"I was going to ask you if there is a way to treat it."

"Treat it, but not cure it. Without a cure the disease, it will eventually attack his brain."

"How can we treat it?" Sam asks.

"There is a formula in the report. I can have it synthesized on Venus."

"Do that for us, but if it's a weapon the Mirancris may have a cure."

"Are you putting that on your list of priorities?"

"The long list, but yes," Sam tells Roczi.

They get on the shuttle, but before Sam goes into the shuttles cargo bay Sam gives one last directive.

"Have the droids set on guard. In case someone managed to follow us."

Sam is wise to be concerned. Off in the distance, someone watches from a cloaked vessel as the ships depart. Inside the hidden luxury spacecraft kilometers away, Suphran scans the station.

"Launch a trace on the station and map its orbit, then take us back to the Infinite," Suphran tells his pilot.

"The Infinite is in Theon hands. There's nothing for us there," The pilot states.

"To question me is to question my plan, and you are not qualified to do either. Just know I have unfinished business there."

"Understood sir," The pilot agrees nervously.

The pilot launches a trace device and maps the stations orbit. They then depart Earth's solar system back to the Infinite's last known location. A location that is currently in enemy hands.

No Strings

In an effort to save time, Sam decides to leave the November at the customs station orbiting Earth and shuttles to London. When he arrives at the UNSA's European headquarters, Sam finds Van Tellure waiting outside of the titanium pillared sky scraper.

"Thank you for getting here so quickly," Zac says to Sam.

"I don't want to keep my best client waiting. Besides, I hope to get better caught up this time."

"I'll be more than happy to catch you up on things, but I don't want to do it here."

"Why is that," Sam asks.

"I'm sick of being in this office, and I need a drink," Zac answers with an uneasy laugh.

"That sounds like a great idea."

The two leave in Van Tellure's Italian sports car for a restaurant near by. Both agree to save the most important talk till they arrive, but small talk in the car is difficult since their minds are so focused on important events. Zac manages to catch Sam up on the activities of the UNSA over the time he's been gone, and Sam catches Zac up on what he's been doing as well. Although, Sam makes sure to leave out small details, like the illegal activities he's been involved in and focuses on exaggerating his shipping and Venusian speaking jobs.

Upon arrival, Sam is relieved to find the restaurant Zac has chosen is an easy going sports themed restaurant, and not something to formal. Although usually fond of them, Sam really just feels like having a few drinks after the extreme nature of recent events. Zac must feel the Sam way.

Once inside they head strait to the bar, where Zac orders a whiskey and Sam a tequila.

"I have to tell you Sam, you made me look damn good getting that information so quickly. My decision to involve you was highly questioned, but the results have left me almost unquestionable. There is very little I can't get done, so if you need anything, now is the time to ask."

"How long do you think it will be before we can develop and use the tech info I acquired?" Sam asks.

"The engineers are already figuring out how to create the devices, and political strategists are coming up with scenarios in witch to use the information. It was a gold mine Sam. It's just to bad the alien ship couldn't be saved. If we had obtained an alien shuttle we could have reversed engineered it's components," Zac says in a way that asks a question.

"I agree, it is a shame, but the report is completely accurate. Have any others made it back from the infinite?" Sam asks trying to change the subject, due to his false report that the shuttle was lost to Saturn's gravity after he failed to understand the ships propulsion.

"Yes some have, and the Mirancris are assuring us they are bringing them back as soon as they can. None appear to have been mistreated."

"What's the ratio coming back?" Sam inquires.

"Approximately one quarter. We're hoping to eventually begin talks with the Theon to get the remaining envoys."

"Is there anything explaining what happened to Lieutenant Niko?"

"No, and it has us questioning wether the Mirancris methods are safe for our people. Everyone is grounded here on Earth till they can prove it is. Another reason it's good to have you around, officially you're not one of our people."

"What's the next step?"

"Getting you back out there to collect as much information as possible. If this information was on a Theon shuttle, there must be more interesting information from the Mirancris."

"If I can find cures for the biowarfare the Mirancris have been using against the Theon it can be leveraged against both species, but especially useful in getting the captured envoys back from the Theon," Sam brings up with Rizac in mind.

"Whatever information you can get is what I'm asking for. I'm empowered to get you just about anything you need. That includes warp tech for the November," Zac tells Sam with a large grin on his face.

Sam's face lights up with the prospect. The thought of what he could do with warp tech on the November would give him a huge edge on the trade routes after his contract with the UNSA is complete. That is, if he manages to complete it alive. Even though Sam already planned on using the Theon shuttle, he knows he could never let Earth's customs see it. Warp tech on the November would allow him to move cargo from Earth and Venus without exposing the discrepancies in his report to the UNSA.

"How long till it's ready," Sam asks.

"We're guessing a week. Take some time to get whatever personal issues you need taken care of. You're gunna be heading into a war zone with aliens we don't trust, doing things they don't want."

"I'm sure I can keep myself alive, but I would appreciate it if you stressed the importance of my return," Sam tells him.

"I'll do what I can Sam, but for right now... lets just see what the locals are watching. I see football, American football, and baseball... Football?" Zac asks.

"I'm the one risking his life out there. We're watching baseball."

"Alright, but you're explaining it to me."

"I'd love to. By the end of the night you will be a huge fan," Sam tells Zac as they let the meeting relax into just another night at a bar.

After the baseball game Sam leaves the bar and takes a flight to his home outside of Phoenix Arizona. There he sleeps one last night at his terrestrial home. The next morning he walks through his house and examines the artwork, electronics, cars, and other luxury items once held so dear. Sam wonders why having these things meant so much to him, then he wonders when his priorities changed.

He has no family, no pets, and no real reason to
return. Sam feels out of his element in his own
home. It's just not where he wants to be. Beyond
that, if things pan out as he wants and expects he
won't be home to often anyway. Sam prefers to be
off the ground, traveling through the newly
discovered systems, feeling the gravitational
anomalies of ships and stations. Just to be a part
of it, is what he wants.

He gathers a few paintings, clothes and
pictures. Then he walks out of his home to a
waiting cab. Sam loads his luggage into the trunk
and walks to the car door. He takes a breath and
one last look at his home.

"Maybe after I retire, but I'm not making
myself any promises," He tells himself.

Sam enters the cab and leaves his home for the
cold comforts of space, and the experiences that
come with it. By the time Sam arrives back at the
Escape Rizac had already began making changes to
the station, and they are already making the It
more livable. Pleased, Sam heads to the bridge
where he finds Rizac.

"You are impressed. I know. Just wait till
Roczi returns with my requested items," Rizac tells
Sam as he enters the bridge.

"I am. Thank you for excepting the position, and once again for getting us out of that situation on that warship."

"I found an opportunity and took it. It happened to work out for both of us."

"Roczi should be here within hours. I'm looking forward to getting her supplies, and seeing what you do with them."

"So you are a fan of skilled, cheap labor. Can't say I blame you."

Roczi arrives two hours later, and informs Rizac that he can unload the shuttle, but then she walks directly to Sam's quarters.

"So Capt. Stix, what is our next move," She asks.

"You have anything that needs to be done? We may be working this contract for a long time," Sam warns her.

"I have some cats at my apartment, but the automation will take care of them."

"You have cats?"

"Yes. Why?"

"Why would you have cats?" Sam asks curiously.

"I enjoy their company. They'll miss me, but I'm ready to go. Unless you would like me to run more errands for you new pal," Roczi says trying to push the conversation forward.

"That reminds me, have we synthesized any medication for Rizac's condition?"

"Yes, but it will only slow the advancement and lessen the pain. Death is inevitable, and impossible to predict."

"Well, lucky for him I moved finding a cure up on my list of priorities."

"Is that our next mission?"

"General Intel is our mission, but I want that cure as leverage. Getting it puts us in a good position."

"What's the plan?" Roczi asks.

"Let the UNSA get us back on a Mirancris ship. That's all I got so far."

"Sounds a little weak to me."

"It does, but right now it's all I got."

Roczi let's out a little sigh, and rolls her eyes in disappointment.

"If you need me I'll be saying bye to my cats."

Roczi leaves the bridge for her quarters, where she can say bye to her cats properly and privately.

Comeback Kid

Suphran returns to the Bigan-Nictwar system in his luxury shuttle, just over an hour away from the Gate's End. Although well within direct sensory range of the Gate's End, he orders his pilot to move in closer, and even turn on a distress beacon. His pilot, begrudgingly does as he's told. By this time all the life shuttles are captured or gone, and the Infinite is occupied by the Theon, but the ship cannot be moved till it's control lock can be breached.

Suphran enters instructions into his communicator and sends.

"Interceptors are incoming," The pilot tells Suphran.

"Put out the surrender signal. Cooperation is the battle plan now."

The interceptors hail Suphran's ship, and direct them toward the Gate's End. He orders his pilot not to respond to the interceptors, but to follow their directives. The next hour should be stressful and tense, but Suphran remains cool and collected. The Theon interceptors lock their weapons on Suphran's luxury spacecraft hoping for a reason to destroy it, but Suphran suspects as much and gives them no reason to fire. When the interceptors reach their target they escort Suphran's luxury vessel into the Gate's End's huge main bay.

Once in the docking bay, Theon soldiers and Laurine mercenaries descend upon the ship and ready their weapons on the doors. Moments pass, then the door opens and the pilot walks out unarmed with his hands out to his sides. A Theon soldier runs up to him and kicks him to the ground.

"Hands behind your back!" The soldier shouts.

A Theon sergeant approaches the ship and begins to shout orders into the door.

"We know there are more of you! Come out now! And please, come out shooting."

Out of the dark doorway, the tell tale red slither of Suphran's skin can be seen, and silence fills the bay. Suphran continues to walkout, and shock freezes the Theon crew to the extent that Suphran actually has to give the first order.

"Sergeant, I believe you should have me restrained," He tells him.

The sergeant looks to the soldier by his side and motions for him to restrain the high level strategist. The soldier approaches him with restraints in hand, and Suphran merely turns his back and extends his hands slowly outward so he can be restrained safely and properly. Once restrained the pilot is taken to the brig while Suphran is held in the bay.

Hidden somewhere on the ship, Kiten continues to make her way through the Gate's End's service corridors. The message Suphran sent included instructions with a target, and Kiten is nearing it now.

On the bridge Captain Threshing still does not know who he has captured till the sergeant notifies him by communicator.

"Captain, I have to inform you of a major development," The sergeant tells Captain Threshing.

"What is it sergeant? I'm still very busy here. I can't imagine why they would lock the ship or come here in the first place."

"Sir, you have just captured General Suphran."

Once again the communicator goes quiet, but this time it's not out of amazement. Captain

Threshing instead uses this time to smile, and arrogantly enjoy his achievement.

Capturing Suphran could mean the war is coming to an end. It would crush Mirancris morale and take there best strategist out of the war.

"Bring the General up to the bridge," Threshing orders.

Suphran is escorted up to the bridge by the security chief and two armed guards. When the shackled Mirancris lead strategist enters the bridge only Captain Threshing is allowed to speak to him.

"So long I've waited for this day General," Captain Threshing says to Suphran.

"What day is that Captain? And please, just Suphran. I'm not a military person, merely a product of necessity."

"Today is the first day of the end of this war."

"Then we have similar goals Captain," Suphran tells Threshing.

"Make no mistake Suphran, this war only ends with the expulsion or eradication of your kind from this system."

After the Captain's statement, Suphran just pauses and looks at him curiously.

"Your kind, eradicating my kind. That is a large goal for such a insignificant species. I wonder what you would do after we're gone Captain. Can you even imagine such a system, or world for that matter? A species created to serve, with no one to serve... A bunch of boot polishers eagerly waiting in lines to polish each others boots! Captain, if your wretched kind does find a way to defeat us, my biggest disappointment would not be that we failed to keep our creation in line. It would be that I missed the comedy of a bunch of feeble minded fools trying to keep up the society we have created," Suphran tells the captain on the brink of laughter.

"Enough of your insults. You must have forgotten, I captured you."

"No Captain. I summoned you," Suphran reminds him.

Angered, Captain Threshing grabs Suphran and takes him to the brig himself. There he begins parading him though the ships prison like a trophy to be displayed. At one point, Threshing stops in the middle of the cellblock to make an announcement from his communicator over the ships warning system.

"I need everyones attention, Mirancris, Human, and Theon..," He announces till he is cut of by Suphran's laughter.

"What could you possibly find so funny?" Threshing asks.

"Nothing. Please go on Captain," Suphran responds as his eyes widen.

Threshing is annoyed by the interruption, but he continues his Announcement.

"The only real hope for the Mirancris war effort has been captured. Your Captain has finished this war..."

Threshing's speech is once again interrupted, but this time it's not by Suphran. An uncontrollable spasm shortly takes control of the captains neck and jaw. A moment later his crew also begin to seize. Then the Captain's seizures worsen, and he falls to the ground. This scene is repeated throughout the Gate's End. Blistered Theon soldiers convulsing on all decks, then dying shortly after.

Suphran crouches low to the ground where Threshing's body continues to convulse. He uses the short time The Captain has left to remind him of his true role in life.

"Your goals are absurd Theon. You are among the best of your kind, and still you fall short.

Did you truly think you could bring your simple
servant species to victory over my mine?" Suphran
says to the dying captain as he removes his
shackles with a device he found on Threshing's
body.

"On the contrary. You have brought demise to
the Theon doorstep," Suphran tells Threshing as he
places his foot on his neck to hasten his death.

He then picks up the dead captain's
communicator and makes an announcement of his own.

"This Vessel now belongs to It's rightful
owners, and will be used for the purpose of
advancing Mirancris interests. Laurine soldiers,
you have failed your contract holders, but I am
willing to give you a second chance. You can show
your allegiance to me by putting down you arms and
reporting to the main conference hall for contract
negotiations, but remember, you are far from home,
and I have many recently released soldiers. Only I
can offer you new contracts."

Suphran makes his leadership clear and
releases the other captured Mirancris, but he
leaves the Human envoys caged in their cells. The
brilliant strategists next order is to go dark and
not communicate with the Infinite, only a few
kilometers off the bow. Then he calls for Kiten to
report to the bridge.

Suphran rushes to meet Kiten, knowing time is their enemy. Suphran needs to take back the Infinite to further his plan. The resources and technology onboard are vital to his war plans. When Suphran arrives at the bridge Kiten is already there waiting.

"Excellent work Kiten, but we are not done."

"What are your orders?" Kiten asks eagerly.

"Take a small team of mercenaries with you to the Infinite. The Theon should not yet know we have taken the ship, so there should not be any fighting involved, but take them armed in case the Theon suspect anything. Get to the life support systems and code them as you did here. It will react with the Theon physiology and produce the same result. Then just wait for my instructions."

"We must move quickly, but I will kill them all," Kiten says as she walks out off the bridge.

"I know you will. That's why I'm sending you."

Reassigned

On the bridge of the escape, Sam sits in his captains chair. Drink in hand and eyes fixed on the main screen, he sips tequila while watching his favorite baseball team. Sam has also been enjoying the wonderful work Rizac has done to the escape. In the last 72 hours the space station has turned into a beautiful and functional place.

The corridors of the station now have marbled brown flooring that appears to slide into a gray or a rust color as you move forward. Art work from Venus, Earth and the Bigan-Nictwar system occasionally appear on the marbled champaign colored walls. As nice as the rooms and corridors are, the bridge is easily Sam's favorite place. True hard wood floors, accented walls and ceilings, with decorative floor boards and crown molding make the bridge look and feel more like something belonging to the East India Company, rather than a twenty-second century space station. Even the different computers and controls have been given a warmer look.

Sam's quarters are still In the same style the Saunders left it. That is why Roczi and Rizac knew to find him on the bridge.

"Sam, we would like your opinion for this discussion," Roczi says as she enters the bridge with Rizac at her side.

"What discussion is this?"

"Rizac wants to give the service corridors and storage areas the same kind of attention the rest of the station has received. I think it's a waste of time and resources."

"Roczi is right. It is a waste of time and resources, but make all the changes you feel necessary Rizac. I'm adding an extra 20,000 credits to your budget for the Escape and the November. We'll wait on the shuttle," Sam tells them.

Rizac and Roczi look at each other. Then Roczi simply shakes her head and remains quiet. Rizac, on the other hand, looks back at Sam and lets out a sound the translation devices could not decipher.

"What was that? My translator didn't get that," Sam tells Rizac.

"I don't know what that was, but I like how you Humans do things," Rizac says as he leaves the bridge.

"What do you think is the hold up with the UNSA? I fully expected to be on an alien vessel by now," Roczi says to Sam.

"So did I Rox. As successful as our last mission was, I figured our assignment would have been given by now."

"Do you think our assignment may have been given to a regular agent?"

"No. Zac would have notified us. We're already being paid, so even if we were being Pushed out they would have found something for us. Even if they just had us patrolling trade routes."

By chance, Sam's communicator goes off just a few minutes later. He answers to hear Zac Van Tellure on the other end. Sam let's out a small sigh of relief as he leans back in his chair and smiles.

Sam stays on the communicator for just over a minute and only speaks a few short questions and responses. Roczi over hears Sam saying things like "Really, What kind of changes?", "This is an unexpected development,", "How do you want me involved?" and "Sounds wonderful. I'll meet you there,".

Whatever Zac told him, Sam was clearly happy with. Immediately after the conversation Sam gets up and begins giving directives. He tells Roczi to

gear up and prep the November, and he let's Rizac
know the Escape is his again. Then Sam starts
walking to the bay where the November is docked,
but stops to gets ahold of Rizac on the
communicator.

"Rizac."

"Yes Sam?"

"If you have the opportunity, could you have
my quarters done in the same style as the bridge?"

Rizac again smiles, enjoying the appreciation.

"I'm sure I'll find the time."

Roczi finishes preparing the November, and
they start their trip to a UNSA station orbiting
Mars. Hours later they see the station off in the
distance. Small for a UNSA station, it's only about
twice the size of the escape and appears to still
be having work done to it. As they get closer they
can see the station is clearly unfinished but must
have all the basic life support systems working.
Onboard the November the ships systems pick up the
hail from the station.

A female voice comes through the ships
communicator in the form of a simple set of docking
instructions. Sam lets Roczi take the November in.
As they dock, Sam and Roczi notice the bay is a
repair station with lots of automated arms on the

walls and ceilings. Seeing this puts ideas in Sam's head and a smile on his face. Roczi realizes she has to rain on Sam's parade just incase he is not getting what they are both expecting.

"Sam don't get your hopes up."

"Oh! Its gunna happen Rox, there is no question in my mind. Stay here with the ship. I got the rest," Sam tells Roczi in a playful manner, nodding his head.

The November's doors open and Sam walks out and into the stations bay. Then a bay door opens, and in walks an exhausted looking Van Tellure. Clearly tired and under pressure, Zac still manages to smile when he sees Sam.

"Glad to have you back Sam."

"Good to see you Zac, but you're not looking so hot."

"I'm fine Sam, I'll be getting plenty of rest by this time next week."

"What do you mean?" Sam asks.

"I'll explain over drinks."

"No thank you Zac. I've had a few..."

"Sam, don't be a bitch. Have a drink with me. I insist," Zac says to Sam.

"Guess I can't argue with the boss," Sam agrees.

The men make their way through the semi built station to what looks like an unfinished bar. Zac explains to Sam that the workers requested the bar be operational for them, and how happy he was to find it operational when he arrived. Especially since earlier in the week Zac had received some bad news.

Whether Zac has always enjoyed his drink or if it is just the current state of events, Sam is enjoying his laid back approach to the systems urgent issues. They share some small talk about Zac's lack of a family life, and Sam's lack of family, as well as other misc topics.

There are a few station workers at the bar, but it remains mostly unoccupied and surprisingly refined. Soon Sam is pleasantly surprised to find a nice looking brunette tending the bar, and she begins making her way toward the two.

"What can I get for you Mr. Van Tellure?" She asks.

"Well Jess, how about your best Bourbon."

"And for you sir?" She asks as she looks to Sam.

"Call me Sam, and I'll have a tequila."

"And keep them coming," Zack adds.

"OK. I'll be right back with your drinks, and then back with more drinks," The bartender says as she walks back to the bar.

Zac Van Tellure looks up and let's out a little gasp, showing fatigue from all the work he's been putting in since the Infinite's arrival. Sam expects a plethora of information to come out of Zac, and he wonders if retaining it all will be a problem, but Sam is accustomed to prioritizing information he is given.

"This is the new situation I mentioned over the com. We were contacted by a Theon representative approximately 24 hours after our last meeting. To put it simply we don't expect them to have anything to offer us. Our military heads believe the only reason they are winning the war is arrogance on the part of the Mirancris. They under estimated the Theon. After reading your report and experiencing the Mirancris for myself, it seems a likely scenario. They simply didn't believe it could happen till it was to late. Funny, since the Theon were all of the security forces and every other type of fighter the Mirancris had."

"A mass disassociation with reality," Sam
adds.

"I'm trying to term it 'hyper advanced
pretension syndrome'," Zac says smiling and shaking
his head.

The Mirancris mind set doesn't take long to
figure out, and already it seems to be rubbing
people the wrong way.

"What are the Theon's goals?" Sam asks.

"They want to prevent a treaty between the
Mirancris and us. We want you to gather information
and see if they have any interest in alliances,
particularly with the A.I.'s."

"I doubt we could suppress an A.I. uprising
now. A synthetic alliance would be frightening, and
possibly unstoppable."

"Yes, that's why if one is coming we need to
know about it. As for us, we have no plans for an
alliance. Our only interest is in advancing
Humanity, and maybe even brokering a peace between
the two species."

"That would leave us in an interesting
position, if both species were positioning for our
favor."

"And that is the position we want. We don't want the A.I.'s to take it. They don't need it. Maybe we don't either, but it does gives us opportunities like the one you just took advantage of."

"How are you getting me in?"

"We are not putting you in the same situation this time. You will be in command of all your movements, and not stuck onboard an alien vessel."

Once again Sam smiles and leans back in his seat. Then the waitress comes by with more drinks.

"I'll be back in a few with more," She tells Sam and Zac.

"Thank you Jessica," Sam says as he gives her a smile.

Jessica notices, and has to smile herself.

"Your smile is infectious," She says to Sam.

"So I have been told, but It's different when you say it."

Her smile broadens as she turns away, but she looks back once more before she returns to the bar.

"Sam, we're still talking here, and I was getting to the best part," Zac tells Sam.

"Sorry Zac. Please continue."

"As we speak the November is being equipped with a Human made warp drive."

"That's what I was waiting to hear. How was it developed so fast?" Sam says excitedly.

"The intel you got us explained everything in detail. In fact this is actually the fourth one we've made, and the second to be installed."

"That is awesome. You should be running the UNSA After the director retires," Sam says raising his glass to him.

"That's what brings me to the bad news. Your success has not gone unnoticed. I have basically been granted permission to do whatever needs to be done, and I am running nearly all diplomatic and intel operations."

"That doesn't sound like bad news."

"It is if your a politician and see me as a future threat. The other heads of the UNSA has decided they don't want me to have this power. As of 1400 hours this afternoon I am merely an adviser. Getting this warp drive to you was one of my last actions."

"Why wouldn't they want you running things? Is it just to keep the director position open for cronies?" Sam asks.

"Maybe, or it could be they don't want a director from the intel division. They didn't come out and say it, but the last meeting had a high diplomacy and exploration tone. Intel and militarization didn't fair nearly so well.

"I'm very sorry to hear that Zac. Is there anything I can do for you?"

"Actually yes," Zac says as he leans back in his seat.

"What is it? Whatever it is I'll get it done."

Zac looks around, then leans in toward Sam.

"Send me all reports at least two hours before you send them to the UNSA. That's all I ask," Zac tells Sam in a whisper.

"Is that it? I was gunna do that anyway."

"Great! And you have a little time on your hands, so have a few more and watch this game with me."

On the big screen is another baseball game, and it takes the two men a few moments for them to realize the players on the screen are machines. Zac is the first to bring up the athletes.

"You know Sam, you are responsible for this."

"What's that Zac? The almost inevitable elimination of Human athletes. I'm not taking credit for that one," Sam says shaking his head.

"You're only partially responsible for that. I'm talking about the mostly carefree peace in the system. We have machines acting Human and playing sports. Oblivious to the gun we have pointed at their heads, and a Human government mostly free of irrational fears. You helped make it all possible. I wouldn't be as confident in our efforts if you weren't involved."

"Neither would I Zac. I'm glad to be onboard," Sam tells Zac as he watches Jessica come back to the table.

As she approaches the table, Sam's focus begins to change from the stability of the system to her bright blue eyes, red lips, and golden brown hair.

Deal Me In

A spacecraft moves slowly and aimlessly through Earth's solar system. It approaches the asteroid belt from the direction of Mars as it's occupants await a destination in an entirely different part of the galaxy. As they drift one of occupants is wondering why.

"You Humans still find ways to keep me guessing," Roczi quietly tells Sam.

"How is that Rox?"

"I'm curious to know how Humanity managed to prosper and advance with such inefficient tendencies."

Sam laughs, then gives Roczi a look from his captains chair.

"Give me an example Rox," Sam asks, even though he knows what she will say.

"We'll, we're basically drifting through space approaching the asteroid belt. I'm guessing for the scenic view. And here we are, still awaiting direction from someone you just left. It would have been simpler just to get it from him in person."

"Rox, where are you getting this nagging behavior?" Sam asks her.

"Well, I haven't had much Human interaction lately, so I've been taking examples from net feed conversations."

"You should stop! That is the worst place to pick up behavior patterns. As for our current situation, if I didn't get out of that bar when I did we would have been severely hindered by my inebriation. This space drift is actually a tactical decision."

"Ah! Good judgment call Sam. I guess not asking for more booze wasn't an option," Roczi says with a light roll of the eyes.

"I prefer this. Besides, they were still working out details with the Theon. How'd the warp drive install go?"

"No issues. I located a tracking device, but I deactivated it."

"I assume the UNSA techs said they knew nothing about it."

"I didn't bother to ask, but I know how you like your privacy. Hey, wait here a moment. I got something for you," Roczi tells Sam.

Roczi then leaves the November's controls and exits the bridge. As the ship gets closer to the asteroid belt Sam gets curious and puts it on the screen. He leans toward the screen and squints slightly. Sam searches the screen, but when he doesn't find what he's looking for he starts to ask the ships computer for a search, but suddenly Roczi returns and Sam abruptly chooses against it.

"Sam, this will help sober you up," Roczi tells him as she hands him a pill and a glass of water.

Sam reaches for the pill and water, but as he does his communicator sounds. Sam leaves Roczi holding her items as he checks his communicator and finds instructions from Van Tellure.

"We just got our instructions. Let's enter the data in the computer and get us there," Sam says.

Roczi sets the glass and pill down next to Sam and clears the ships main screen for a map of their destination. Sam and Roczi are heading back to the Bigan-Nictwar system.

"All systems go Sam. The warp drive is ready."

"How should I say it Rox? I want this term used in all Human vessels."

"That's entirely up to you Sam."

Sam looks around the bridge a bit, then sets his eyes forward on the screen.

"Initiate."

Roczi turns from the helm, and looks at Sam.

"That's a bit lame," She tells him

"Just get us there Rox."

Roczi complies with the order and brings the November into warp. The bridges main screen displays what appears to be be space bending in front of them, and an automated voice gently announces the event. From the outside of the November, the ship quickly leaps forward into warped space, and suddenly disappears. Then, just outside of a planetary system in an entirely different part of the galaxy, space bends just as it did in Earth's system, but here the November appears out of nothing moving just under the speed of light. Only a moment had passed, but many light years had been traveled. Now Sam and Roczi may continue their mission in the warring system.

It's impossible to navigate within an area as small as a solar system at warp, so the November

must use it's conventional engines for the
remaining duration of the trip. This leaves plenty
of time for Roczi and Sam to check the map of the
system for discrepancies and possible threats.

The system is small in comparison to Earth's,
with only 4 planets, but they are comparable. The
first planet closest to its sun is called Demav,
and it is remarkably similar to Venus. It is a
rocky planet with a dense atmosphere, and a surface
temperature to hot for organic life. The final
planet furthest from their sun is a gas giant
slightly larger than Jupiter. It's name is Unscern.
It credits the system with eight moons. Three of
those moons are inhabited by Mirancris or Theon,
but the real jewel of the system are the planets of
Bigan and Nictwar.

Bigan is the original home planet of the
Mirancris. It is covered with old towering
structures, thousands of massive lakes, and tens of
thousands of rivers. The short green and blue
vegetation, and white clouds give the planet a
light turquoise color. The Mirancris still hold
control of the planet as the Theon focused on it's
vastly more industrial sister planet.

The second planet of this binary system is
Nictwar. This planet has only been inhabited for
two-hundred-thirty-seven years but it is the most
advanced planet in the known galaxy. Before
Mirancris settlers inhabited the planet it was
nearly a mirror image of Bigan, but now it is a

planet of new towering silver and black structures, and clear shallow pools. Previous to colonization plant life had already made it to Nictwar, presumably from Bigan, while animal and sentient life arrived after colonization. The planet is currently under complete control by Theon rebels, but most of its industrial complexes are not operational since very few Theon were made for logistics, finance, or engineering. Still, the few factories that are manufacturing arms and other goods are putting out numbers only seen by factories labored by Venusian machines.

Sam is en route to a location about 30 thousand Kilometers off Nictwar. All of this systems space stations were destroyed at the start of the war, so a giant luxury ship turned warship is where Sam will meet the Theon dignitary.

As they near the rendezvous point, the first thing the November's sensors pick up are the giant steel plates suspended around the ship. The ship is substantially smaller than the Gate's End but similar in design, and as Roczi pilots the November toward the vessel they receive a hail.

"November this is Guide. Please acknowledge."

"Guide, this is the November. We hear you and are en route to your location. Please provide further instructions," Roczi responds.

"Please begin your approach and prepare to dock November."

"Negative Guide. I am prepared to drop off Captain Stix, but this vessel is to remain in orbit and in my command during his absence.... Do you copy Guide?"

A few moments pass, then the Guide sends another transmission.

"We copy November. You will be receiving a map and coordinates. You can drop off your envoy at that location."

"Understood Guide."

On the screen, a ship can be seen leaving the Guide. It carries the Theon dignitary heading for a destination on Nictwar. A few moments later the map and destination appear on the November's computer.

"How are we picking up their transmissions?" Sam asks.

"From a simple format translator."

"Are our systems safe?"

"Our systems don't read it. It's only a com translation. No programs can possibly be ran."

Happy with Roczi's work, Sam gives her a little nod and smile.

"Thank you," He tells her.

"Whatever you need Sam. I'm happy to be here for you."

"Take me to the destination. Stay on constant monitoring as you orbit the planet. I'll contact you with further instructions."

"I will. Sam, be careful."

"I'll be fine. The Theon are trying to prevent an alliance, not provoke one."

Sam and Roczi arrive above a very large city, over a massive building, with a roof top large enough for both the Theon shuttle and the November. The November descends to a near landing, only centimeters above the rooftop.

Already standing alone beside a spacecraft much larger than the November is the Theon dignitary, but this Theon is different from the ones Sam has seen before. He is smaller, much smaller. The dignitary stands only about a meter and a half tall and appears to be thin and frail. Wearing a draping silky black robe, he looks nothing like the massive Captain Threshing or the towering Rizac. This Theon looks more like a malnourished reject, as opposed to a capable work horse. If not for the circumstances, Sam would have thought he encountered an entirely different alien species.

The Theon dignitary approaches the November as it hovers just above the roof top. Sam exits down the ramp and watches the nonthreatening alien standing only meters away. Then an expression of awe comes across the Theon's face as Sam walks down the ramp.

"I recognize you. I am surprised to see you here in front of me," The alien dignitary tells Sam.

"Why is that?" Sam asks.

The two walk away from the November as Roczi slowly and quietly takes her into orbit.

"I recognize you from a report sent by Captain Threshing of the Gate's End. The report pictured and stated that you were being brought to Nictwar as a prisoner."

"Yes, that is a fact. I'm impressed that you mentioned my unlawful imprisonment," Sam tells him.

"I think the truth is a good place for our people to start a relationship. I am Fomn."

"Well Fomn, since we're being honest I have to tell you, you're not what I expected from a Theon."

Fomn laughs.

"I'll have answers to all your questions once we get inside. On this side of Nictwar high tide is coming, and high tide brings random attacks from Bigan."

The two walk to a lift on the rooftop. Then It takes them down steadily.

"I assume you expected someone larger like every other Theon you've met," Fomn tells Sam as they descend into the building.

"Yes. I get the impression you weren't designed for physical labor."

"No. Although illegal to create Theon for things other than laborious tasks, money had lifted a few wealthy Mirancris above the law."

"That sounds interesting. Please explain."

"Some wealthy Mirancris business executives, like my former superior, found they could retire without retiring if they had proper benefactors. During the Mirancris evacuation of Nictwar, near the beginning of the revolt, we were left behind, expelled from Bigan, or killed. So now I am part of the council on logistics, with an emergency added assignment of joint Theon/Human interests."

"That is interesting. Fomn, I'm curious how the war has effected the inhabited moons around the Unscern?" Sam asks.

"The moons are simply unimportant to us at this time. From what I understand the war has hurt their economies, but they are running like nothing is even going on. They are not killing each other. I wouldn't recommend basing normal life on what goes on in the systems outer settlements. It is very different."

From the rooftop, they descend down an elevator directly into a large office, where the two walk off the lift. Then Sam inquires about Fomn's earlier comments about high tide attacks.

Fomn points to one of the office windows and Sam steps toward it. There he sees small explosions on the rooftops and streets of the city.

"More of an irritation than an attack really. The weak gravity of high tide makes it possible for average citizens, and even children, to fire munitions from one planet to the other. They're having the same irritation on Bigan as we speak."

"Shouldn't the rockets still take weeks to arrive?" sam asks.

"Normally, but These toys are equipped with warheads and weak NLS tech, Curtesy of the Mirancris government.

The weak gravity is noticeable to Sam. The gravity is actually so weak Sam feels as if he can jump to the next floor, and probably up two floors with suit enhancements. This leaves Sam with another question, how miserable will low tide feel?

"I do have some questions for you Sam. The Gate's End was in the act of capturing the Infinite when we last heard from Capt. Threshing, then they both just disappeared without a trace. Since you we're there could you provide us with some insight on what may have occurred?"

"When I escaped from the Gate's End, Threshing was in complete control. I figured both ships and any Human occupants were in Theon custody."

"I wish I could say they were, but we were concerned that we lost both ships due to some kind of Human intervention."

"I can promise you Humanity has in no way entered this war," Sam tells Fomn with certainty.

"I am happy to hear that. It wouldn't make much sense for a third party to intervene."

"Has there been any sign of debris from the ships. Vessels that large would have left a noticeable debris field."

"The guide has searched with several other vessels for several days. Nothing has been found."

"So it's possible the Human diplomats are in Mirancris custody, and they haven't notified the UNSA."

"If you don't mind ambassador Stix, I would like to inform the other councilors of this new information."

"And I would like to notify The UNSA as well. Can we continue this another time? This type of information can't wait," Sam says to Fomn.

"I agree. I think Humanity needs to know that we are not holding any one, and it should be known as soon as possible."

At this point both Sam and Fomn go their own ways to inform their peers and superiors of this new information. Fomn disappears deeper in the massive building, and Sam heads back to inform the UNSA that the answers he came here for have left them with more questions.

Enlightened Confusion

From the rooftop of the building Sam can see the planet Bigan in the sky. The small rockets coming from it and the small explosions they cause can also be seen throughout the once great city.

Roczi notifies Sam that she is nearing the roof top, so Sam turns his attention to the sky to find her. He watches the November as she approaches. Her steely grey outer skin, and white under-glow can be seen as she descends into the atmosphere. Sam realizes this is the first time he has seen the November on approach. He now puts his life in Roczi's hands in an almost complacent manner, but instead of being concerned by this rationalization Sam is happy knowing he has found someone he can trust.

Roczi once again doesn't bother to drop the landing gear as she reaches the roof top. She just drops the ramp and Sam walks onboard.

"Get us home Rox. We need to get this report to Zac and the UNSA," Sam says as he enters the bridge.

"How did the meeting go Sam?"

"It was informative and very concerning."

"Concerning? How was it concerning?"

"The Theon say they aren't in control of the Gate's End or the Infinite, but according to the Mirancris neither are they."

"We were on the Infinite and the Gate's End as the Theon decisively took it. I don't see how the Mirancris could have possible retaken the ship, let alone taken them both," Roczi tells Sam with a curious look.

"A ship as war ready as The Gate's End would not have let a luxury ship like the Infinite take her down."

"However you look at it, there are still people missing or being held captive. The UNSA may even believe an act of war has been committed," Roczi says with a serious expression.

Sam takes a seat in his captains chair then looks at Roczi.

"Well Rox, if my people need my formidable skill set you may see the darker side of my training. I'm talking battalions of alien enemy combatants dead by my hand," Sam jokingly tells Roczi.

"I hope not Sam. You seem in over you head as it is, but I'll always be there to steer you through it," Roczi replies with an equal amount of cynicism.

Vast distances away from any of the known inhabited systems is an freezing purplish planet with two natural moons. It is a large ice planet with different types of alien plant life on the steep walls of its frozen canyons. Now two huge superstructures are also orbiting the planet, but the Infinite and Gate's End are not in orbit for the planets scenic views.

On the surface of the planet are many squads of Laurine mercenaries. They are on a mission to capture different forms of life. The Laurine's eight limbs make them excellent for maneuvering on the canyon walls. They can be seen climbing through the steep canyons with their weapons ready and carrying gear, but still easily Maneuvering along the walls. The creatures these mercenaries capture are caged then shuttled to the infinite for study by Mirancris bioengineers and weapon engineers.

Several species are showing promise to the Mirancris scientists, but one is showing more than most during initial tests. It's a short, stocky, spike-scaled, bipedal predator with forward binocular vision and the ability to manipulate objects with it's hands. The creatures only apparent downfall is it's lack of intelligence, but Suphran's lead bioengineer, Doctor Minger, is more than willing to make the necessary changes to turn this creature into a soldier. Even so, the scaled, bipedal, predator's physical characteristics are not what makes it so special. It's brain activity shows that it is in a constant state of pain. This pain is felt all its life, but in times of distress it's glands produce a type of pain-killer, and a chemical that increases focus, speed, and reaction time. This makes the beast seek-out and enjoy dangerous situations.

Although impressive to Suphran's weapon engineers, interest in S.B.P-1 has been surpassed in the eyes of lead bioscientist, Doctor Minger, by a much more primitive species.

Suphran and Kiten are walking to the Infinite's science labs to learn what is so astonishing Doctor Minger wants to show Suphran before he describes it in his report. As the door to the lab opens the excitement within is obvious within.

"What is this breakthrough you need to show me Dr. Minger?" Suphran asks.

"Come with me and look," Doctor Minger replies.

The doctor walks a few meters to a large glass wall, and pushes others out of the way so Suphran can see. Kiten, being a meter taller than even the tallest Mirancris in the room, stays back aways utilizing her natural vantage point.

Beyond the glass is a very large sunken room, and in the middle is a three meter tall, dark grey humanoid machine covered with what looks like flesh. Then the Doctor enters a code into a control panel, and a large door opens on the other side the sunken room. From the large door enters a large grey creature, that seems to be infused with machines.

In an instant the more machine of the two creatures attacks the more biological. The two creatures fight. They punch, wrestle, and toss each other around the arena. The more biological of the two creatures is injured, but it quickly heals itself, where the more mechanical only has enhanced abilities and durability. The beasts fight for over 10 minutes, but in the end the creature forces the machine into it's slower paced fight. The creature beats the machine by bogging it down and picking it apart, but Suphran is not as impressed as expected.

"Nice doctor, but why couldn't this have been given to me in a report?" Suphran asks.

"The two samples you witnessed were created within hours of each other. We found a creature who's cells work independently but cooperatively. Each cell communicates with the others and moves nutrients and information to other cells. The cells work similar to a hive, putting the needs of the group before the individual cell. They morph themselves into whatever they need, including thick protective armor, and can even replace the cells of a creatures dead native cells. Keeping trauma victims alive."

"It is very interesting but why did you need me to be witness this. A report would have been sufficient."

"Suphran a report would have been late. These creatures were not just created quickly, they adapt quickly. They've already adapted themselves to survive in space without atmosphere. The room they were battling in is void of air. They were fighting in the vacuum. There are developments going on in this lab that happen to quickly to report... They..."

"Stop further creature development now," Suphran interrupts.

"I will not have our previous mistakes bite us a second time in the name of pride or progress. For the time being, we will only create the army we now know and supplement it with S.B.P.-1 samples. I do

not want further development with the hive cells as
of yet."

"Yes Suphran," Doctor Minger replies after a
short dissatisfied pause.

"Doctor Minger, create several squads of Theon
soldiers, and have the intelligence officer
interrogate the Humans we have. If possible, take
the memories from their corpses."

Suphran then turns his attention to Kiten and
tells her to meet with him on his shuttle. Suphran
then leaves the room and Doctor Minger begins to
follow, but Kiten grabs his shoulder.

"Doctor, Did you say the cells can replace an
organism's dead tissue, and keep it alive?" Kiten
asks.

"Yes, why."

"There was a Human solider found dead, or
dying in an envoys quarters. What is his status?"

"He was found in the earliest stages of death,
but the tissues were still in near perfect
condition. The body is being preserved in cryo.
Again, why?"

"Suphran may not have put priority on the hive
cells, but I think we could use them and the human

to determine Human combat tactics. I want him alive, and programmable. Can you do this?

"Theoretically yes, but Suphran has work on the cells on hold."

"Where does it sit on your list of priorities Doctor? I assure you other scientists on this vessel will be working with the cells. You don't want to fall behind," Kiten tells the doctor, not bothering to hide her manipulation.

"I can bring him back just as you want, and it won't take long."

"Remember, intact and controllable. Contact me with his progress."

"I should have the Human ready within days."

"Very good."

Shortly thereafter, Suphran and Kiten board his luxury shuttle and leave the safety of the Infinite for the warring space of the Bigan-Nictwar system. The head the of Mirancris war effort is heading back to inform the leadership that he has a different plan to end the war and save his people, but it in no way involves them.

"Take me home Kiten. This will be a very short round trip."

"What is your plan Suphran?"

"I'm doing this in stages. The first stage is to stop the onslaught and let my species regroup."

"How will you do that?"

"By forcing unwanted involvement," Suphran quickly replies.

Their shuttle leaves the small distant system, en route to Suphran's warring home system. When the shuttle arrives at their destination it stays on the system's outskirts. There they are less likely to be noticed, but still well within communications range.

"Kiten, would you get Vycelar Hilks on the com?"

"Yes, he'll be on momentarily."

Kiten connects Suphran to Vycelar Hilks, the head authority of Bigan's Unified Government. Answering his communicator, the Vycelar is overjoyed to see Suphran has returned. The hopes of Mirancris survival fall on the shoulders of this one individual. The species feels he is the most promising hope for the the Mirancris.

"Suphran! I thought you were gone! There will be spontaneous celebrations throughout the planet once they hear you're alive."

"You may want to keep my reemergence quiet, and look for a new head of strategy and logistics," Suphran tells Hilks.

There is a pause followed by a changing of the Vycelar's eye's. He squints and the outer corners of his eyes flare slightly forward. A clear sign of Mirancris anger.

"Why would you do this? Betray and abandon us. Do you know how this will effect your people?"

"I've lost hope in the old Mirancris strategy. I'm starting new, creating a plan more proficient in design to give us the system. Please, feel free to tell the people what you want, or what they need to hear. I'm just letting you know, as of now you'll need to fight the war without me."

"You can't abandon your duties Suphran!"

"I'm doing what's necessary Vycelar Hilks. Good luck to you."

Suphran disconnects from the Vycelar and just sits there looking at his screen, taking in what may be his last look at his home.

"Suphran, are you truly abandoning the Mirancris?" Kiten asks.

"Take us back to the Infinite Kiten," Is all he says.

Kiten asks no other questions. Confused and curious to his plan she follows his order.

Once the November arrives back in Earth's system, Sam quickly gets Van Tellure on the communicator.

"Zac, I've got a huge development for you."

"What is it Sam?"

"The Theon are telling me they do not have any Human envoys, the Gate's End, or the Infinite."

"The ships and all who occupy them are unaccounted for?" Zac states as a question.

"Fomn seemed sincere as he told me. He even brought up how I was supposed to have been taken to the planet as a prisoner. Still he could just be trying to gain our trust."

"I'm at a loss. Can you think of any reason either species would hold our people, or deny being in control of the capitol ships?"

"I can think of a dozen reasons, and so can you. Zac, I'd hate to be in your shoes right now."

"This is confusing and unexpected. Thank you for telling me first. There are a few new developments on our end, but mostly tech. Give me two hours before you let the rest of the UNSA know."

"Whatever you need Zac. Talk soon."

Sam turns off the communicator and looks back at Roczi.

"We have approximately four hours and probably not much more. I'd like to get more armament from the Escape," Sam tells Roczi.

"Armament? Why would we need more weapons Sam?"

"I don't trust any of these aliens, and I won't allow myself to fall into a bad situation unprepared."

"Understood. Let's gear up."

Roczi then sets their course once more for the Escape.

Contact Control

Once back at the Escape, Rizac coordinates the move of three of the six combat droids, as well as food, munitions and other supplies onto the November.

"I knew you were bringing weapons, but don't you think the droids are a bit much?" Roczi asks Sam.

"I have this feeling things are barely being kept in control by either of the alien's leadership. I don't want us in a position where we find ourselves under equipped."

"I was surprised you two came back so soon. I was looking forward to having the station to myself a little longer," Rizac tells them.

"We'll be out before to long. You may even miss us a bit before we return," Roczi says to Rizac.

Sam is pleased to see the relationship between Roczi and Rizac becoming friendly after the cold start. Rizac's new surrounding have clearly made a positive impact on his outlook and attitude, and Sam appreciates the better all around environment and loyalty having a happy crew brings.

"Sam, since you'll be leaving soon I want to give you a gift," Rizac tells Sam.

"Great... Where can I check it out?" Sam says with a mixture of sarcasm and curiosity.

"This cargo bay will be fine."

Rizac then reaches into his coat and pulls out Sam's gift with what may be considered a smile on his face. He is clearly proud of his gift, and although Sam is interested, his communicator goes off so he puts off Rizac's gift.

"Hold on a moment Rizac. I have a message from the UNSA."

Sam is a little disappointed that it's just directions to another docking station telling him to pick up some equipment and more directions, but his eagerness to get started and curiosity cause

Sam to speedily start boarding the November, and forget about the gift Rizac has for him.

"Sam! This won't take long! Give me just a moment," Rizac shouts at Sam, trying to get him to look at the gift he has designed for him.

"I'll look at it when we get back," Sam tries to tell Rizac, but when he sees it he stops immediately.

Rizac points to the gift in his hand and a 1.25 meter long white plasma blade, with a red half meter long charged disruptor core swiftly appears from it. Sam's gift is a peijax.

Sam's face lights up with renewed interest. He walks back down the November's ramp to examine his new toy."

"That is amazing," Sam tells Rizac, impressed by the blade.

"It looks different from mine cause I specified it for you. The white is the cutting and killing part, and the red is the defensive part of the blade. The killing part is self explanatory, and the red is charged to disrupt plasma and repulse matter."

"Nice! I'll take it now. You can show me how to use it later."

"Do you mean training? That's not my roll on this station. You can figure out how you want to use it on your own. I'm glad you like it, but if things get difficult, use a gun," Rizac tells Sam as he turns and walks back to the bridge.

Roczi and Sam board the November and leave for the UNSA station. After several hours the November arrives at the space station and docks. There they find a UNSA agent waiting for them.

"I'm Agent Ken Marx," The agent tells Sam.

"Sam Stix."

"Well then, we have the S.S. and K. Marks in one room."

"We may pose a serious threat to western civilization," Sam says jokingly.

The two men share a brief laugh at the comedic reference to the twentieth centuries prominent reasons for war and rebellion. Then they continue with their real business.

"Sam, I'm your new contact. Any information you obtain will from now on be sent via warpcom to me without having to warp back to our system."

"Warpcom? Please explain," Sam asks.

"It's really just small automated warp system drone used to keep communications private. The initial idea was to have them track and travel to each agents ship, but that left pick up work for the agents. So now they are all one way drones, from the agents to the contacts. I'm sure the real reason is our agents would rather not be tracked."

"I would have to agree with your latter assumption. The UNSA worked very fast to accommodate their agents. Seems a bit out of character."

"It also helps prevent the preferential dispersion of information. Mr. Stix, You have to understand the latest changing of roles was necessary. It is in Humanities best interest."

"And all this time I thought it was in the politicians best interest," Sam tells Marx cynically.

"Your assignment is the same. The only change is if you have any info that needs to be sent to the decision makers you don't have to leave. It will save you a hell of a lot of time. We have droids waiting to load the warpcoms as we speak."

"People are missing and you call me back so the UNSA can put a leash on me."

"There are people missing whether we call you back for a leash, or if you give Van Tellure advanced notice. The clock tics either way."

"I'm just a contractor. Those are your people missing, and you're supposed to be taking care of them. I'd expect better from the agency," Sam says, full knowing his argument is rife with hypocrisy and poor logic.

"It is how it is. Hope to hear from you soon Sam."

Agent Marx then leaves, and two droids enter the bay with dozens of cylindrical warpcoms. After the droids bring the warpcoms onto the November Sam leaves the station and sends Van Tellure a message. He advises Zac that the new communications situation will prevent him from sending advanced notice, and that he's going back to Nictwar and Councilor Fomn.

Several hours later Sam is back on a rooftop in the Theon held planet of Nictwar, but Fomn is not there to greet them. Instead another large Theon is there with a message and more equipment.

"Sam Stix, Councilor Fomn will not be able to meet with you tonight, but we have made arrangements for your stay till tomorrow," The Theon tells Sam.

"That is fine. I would prefer a night of relaxation, and a little time to get acquainted with my new surroundings."

"Excellent. These items will help you with your navigation and in finding places of interest. You will find transportation and a driver on the third level."

"Great. More equipment. Now all I need is more storage space," Sam says sarcastically.

"I'm sorry, did you say you needed something else?" The Theon asks Sam.

"No. No. I'll just go to my hotel for now. Maybe I'll do some sight seeing tomorrow."

The two continue an awkward conversation about several non-related ideas and how they could effect the wars outcome as they walk to an elevator. The conversation makes Sam wonder why they are even talking. After all, quite is preferred to displayed ignorance. Another awkward moment occurs as Sam enters the elevator with the Theon equipment and the door begins to shut between the two. The Theon continues to speak his nonsense as the doors shut and the elevator descends. Sam leaves his host on the roof top, where he is likely still flapping his gums (or what he has in place of them). The incident amuses Sam and brings a smile to his face. The smile develops into a laugh as he approaches the third floor.

"Roczi, did you see that?" Sam asks laughing, knowing Roczi is watching through his suits embedded sensors.

"Yes I did. I'm still wondering why he didn't just get in the elevator with you," Roczi tells Sam through his earpiece.

"Once I get to the hotel I'm putting the sensors on the Theon equipment so we can replicate it and get it's information."

"Always on task in your own special way Sam. I do love that about you."

"Roczi, your emulation of love is more than this man could ask for."

"You know just what to say to keep a girl emulating. My processors are firing slightly warmer for you."

"I cant believe I'm flirting with you. I need to meet a girl Rox," Sam says smiling.

Roczi laughs a bit before responding.

"Oh, come on Sam. We were having fun, besides you're good at it."

"You still out shine me there Rox, but I'll accept the compliment."

The elevator comes to a stop and the door opens. The third level appears to be a parking platform that leads directly out to several levels of holographic lanes. A Theon driver only moderately larger then a Human and dressed in all black is there waiting. He informs Sam that his name is Loman and that he will take him wherever he wants to go, but at the moment Sam is only Interested in getting to his hotel. Once there he will begin delivering the information gained from the alien devices.

The commute to the hotel is quick, and there are very few vehicles seen flying through the holographic sky lanes. The Theon and Mirancris call the holographic sky lanes "light lanes", and they are noticeably empty for what looks like a once a great city.

They arrive at the hotel and the driver notifies Sam that he will be there whenever he needs him, and more than happy to take him throughout the city. Sam thanks him. Then a hotel employee quickly arrives to show him to his room.

Sam is happy to see Fomn has acquired a very nice room for him. It's a penthouse near the top of a building with a wonderful view of the city.

"Well Rox, I'm in the room and setting up the sensors on the alien devices," Sam tells Roczi using his suits sensors.

"I'll be waiting for it Sam. Is there anything I can do to make your stay a little nicer?"

"Send me some ball game feeds," Sam requests as he prepares the sensors to start sending information to Roczi.

Once finished Sam sits on a couch and places a halo-projector on a table next to him. He pops a sleep aid into his mouth and waits for the projector to start. Once it does he verbally requests to catch up on some of the baseball games he had missed. Then he allows himself to slowly drift off to sleep, and miss them again.

Getting Involved

Explosions Ring out the next morning, abruptly waking Sam. The explosions are a bit of shock, but the realization that baseball games are still playing on his projector also surprises him.

"Wow, I missed more games than I thought," Sam tells himself out loud.

Sam's communicator begins to signal as he gathers himself. He answers the communicator to hear the very familiar voice of Roczi on the other end.

"Sam, there are fire fights popping off throughout the city, and I picked up cloaked ships going through the atmosphere."

"Any danger to you or the November?" Sam asks.

"I've moved back and engaged the cloak. I should be safe."

"In that case, keep track of things for me while I take a shower."

"Do you want me to pick you up Sam?"

"No. I don't want you or the November in harms way, and I still want to have my meeting with Fomn as planned."

"I doubt Fomn will be willing to meet with you during a battle."

"I don't plan on giving him a choice. I want to see how Theon strategists are winning this war. It can be valuable intel."

"Your call Sam. It's a bad call, but good luck."

Sam is happy to find the hotel happens to be somewhat Human friendly. It only takes Sam a few minutes to figure out the the shower controls. After a quick shower Sam is in full gear and heading back to the vehicle where Loman will hopefully be waiting and willing to drive.

Sam is relieved to find he is there just like he said he would be.

"Mr. Stix, I can still take you wherever you want to go, but I must tell you, the attack has made most of the city center much more dangerous," Loman tells Sam.

"Can you take me to Fomn?"

"I can take you there, but the building is under siege. You won't get in to speak with him."

"Can you get ahold of him for me?"

"I can't, but you have a communicator in the equipment you were given."

Sam takes a look at a hand held device and finds a communicator feature. It too is similar to his own, and although he cannot understand the script, it is setup to go directly to Fomn.

"Fomn! I'm glad I was able to get a hold of you."

"Stix, this is an inopportune time to speak. The city is under attack."

"Yes, but I'm under the impression your forces have this under control."

"Not yet, but they will soon. I'm still trying to figure out what the Mirancris hope to gain from this offensive."

"I'm en route to your location."

There is a short quiet pause as Fomn questions what he just heard.

"You Humans are odd, but as long as your assistant will clear us of liability, you can make all the poor decisions you want. You will encounter tough resistance trying to reach me in the tower. I'll Instruct my security forces not to kill any Humans," Fomn says with a small laugh.

"I appreciate the assistance... Is there any information you can give me that will help?"

"Yes. You should stay in your suite till the battle is over."

"Something that will help me reach you."

"If you insist...The attacking forces are lead by Mirancris and Laurine, but the bulk of the forces are newly made first generation Theon. You will have to distinguish the Mirancris slave force from our fighters by uniform. I'll send you the description and my location. I hope to see you alive."

Disappointed, Fomn closes communications and sends the information to Sam.

"Loman, how close can you get me to the building?" Sam asks.

"I can safely get you within half a kilometer of the building. Keep an eye out for patrols."

"You're not a typical driver are you?" Sam says curiously.

"I used to drive for a mob boss before the war. I was literally made for this."

Loman takes off quickly, and moves fast three stories over the city's floor. Patrols can be seen on the roads firing at the vehicle, but a single vehicle is not what they came here for. The driver shows off his skills, hugging corners and the tall buildings. Loman pushes the vehicle to it's limits. Finally the vehicle pulls into a steep climb then begins to slow twelve stories high. Pulling up as close to a building as he can Loman finds a balcony and parks just above it.

"How's this?" The driver asks.

"It's good. Thanks for the ride."

"Remember me when you come back to visit."

"I will," Sam says as he jumps out and on to the balcony.

Once he enters the building and Loman pulls away, Sam gets a situation report from Roczi.

"What should I expect Rox."

"The info Fomn is sending is current and in real time. The invaders are camouflaged in basic urban camo, but the special squads are in light refracting suits made up of Laurine and Mirancris. I am sending you the location info, and I will be monitoring your advance."

"What's the best way in," Sam asks.

"Go down to the fourth floor, then directly across the building and enter Fomn's building by jumping across to the 3rd floor."

"Why the third floor?"

"The bottom floor is secured by Mirancris forces and the higher levels are being monitored by their special squads looking for Theon trying to escape. Infiltration from the third floor and moving up through the center of the building is your best option."

"They may be looking for people trying to get out but I'll make a pretty noticeable target flying through the air between buildings."

"You're the one who insisted on meeting with Fomn this morning. I thought you were just going to have me send a report to the UNSA. Besides, the buildings are very close. If they can react and hit you in the time it takes to jump from one building to another, then we will know you should have stayed at the hotel."

"Report...Looking back now, that would have been the smart thing to do," Sam says as he runs down several flights of stairs

Sam arrives at a long corridor with a large window at the end. He then looks out the window to the third story of Fomn's building. Sam then takes several steps back and brings out his trident pistol.

"Sam... You know you can't open fire on those soldiers. This isn't our war."

"I have no intention of bringing myself into this war. I just think this set of circumstances may bring valuable intel, or show Human commitment toward peace. This bad idea may prove to be very important."

After that Sam starts sprinting toward the window. He fires one shot breaking both his fourth floor window and the adjacent third floor window. He leaps through the still shattering glass and dives through the air into the next building's third floor window. After a tuck and roll, then an unintentional second roll and flop, Sam stands up and collects himself.

"You still there Rox?"

"Run Sam! Run!"

The urgency In her voice sends Sam scrambling down a corridor away from the shattered window. The images Roczi picks up from Sam's sensors show a squad quickly converging on His location.

Immediately after Sam began running through the corridor a flying troop transport closes in on the window. Mirancris soldiers with Laurine mercenaries begin jumping from their troop transport through the window. Sam runs further down the hall trying to elude his pursuers. He turns down another corridor and runs a couple offices down. There, Sam finds an early use for his peijax when he comes to a door and uses it to cut through it's lock.

"Send a message to the UNSA letting them know our situation, but not telling them how I got into it. I'll keep trying to work my way up to Fomn," He tells Roczi.

"Trying to justify hazard pay? Sending the warpcom now. You need to stay away from the elevators they have been shutdown and I'm sure they are being monitored."

"What's the best way up?" Sam asks Roczi.

"Through the ceilings and floors."

"Can't I take the stairs."

"There are no stairs."

Sam thinks to himself, "Who makes a building without stairs?" Then he enters the office. He takes his peijax and slices into a ventilation shaft and starts climbing his way up fast. Sam expects the Mirancris to quickly make chase. Every time Sam looks down the shaft he thinks he will see a Laurine pursuer climbing up after him, but there are none. Sam climbs till he sees more vents. Believing the vents will lead him into another room Sam cuts his way through, but he finds himself entering another corridor.

He tries to get Fomn on the alien communicator but it fails. Then Sam tries to reach Roczi, but it too fails. Then around the corner and down the hall he hears what sounds like something creeping. Then down the hall in the other direction he hears the same thing. Other than these two small sounds it is perfectly quite. Then the silence is once again broken.

"Stop there. Don't move."

Sam hears a voice come though the hall. Sam freezes then looks, but he still sees nothing. The hall is dim, but there is enough light to see all the way down both ways. Sam slowly backs against the wall.

"I said don't move. I will kill you."

This time Sam notices a slight bass with knocks and hums. The sound of of true Mirancris speech.

"Shackle it," Sam hears.

Then the tell tale warped image of a creature in light refracting camouflage stands up. From the hight and thin area of altered light Sam can tell the creature is Laurine. The Laurine approaches Sam and pulls out a set of restraints. Sam prepares himself to fight, but the sound of something moving down the hall stops the Laurine in it's tracks. The next thing to be heard is the wisp of projectiles flying through the air hitting bodies and corridor walls. Sam dives back into the shaft to avoid getting killed.

The fighting only takes a few seconds, then the quite returns. There was no screaming as they died. Just the thud of bullets hitting bodies.

Sam can only wait in the shaft now. A minute passes that seems like an hour, but nothing moves. Then Sam again begins to hear things stirring in the hall. It's the sound of something slowly creeping his direction. Sam is grabbed without warning and pulled back into the corridor, but he does not resist. Sam realizes at this point that his best chance at survival is not to give anything a reason to kill him.

Puzzle
Pieces

Just pulled out of the ventilation shaft, Sam
is quickly dragged through one corridor to another,
than another. The soldier dragging Sam is large,
strong, and unmistakably Theon. He is finally taken
into a room with a large hole in the ceiling. Sam
is brought directly under the hole, where he sees
more large holes in the ceilings going sixty
stories strait up. They close the door to the
office and their camouflage deactivates into a more
typical black uniform.

A cable is fired from someone above down
through the holes, and a soldier quickly anchors
the cable to the floor. One of the Theon soldiers
takes Sam's right hand and attaches a device to it.
The device resembles a wrist brace with a pair of
hooks near the back of his hand.

"Cable between the hooks," The soldier tells
Sam.

Sam looks at the cable and sees tiny waves of light traveling up the cable. By simply placing his wrist near the cable he sees the small light waves reach out from the cable and connect to the hooks. All of the sudden Sam is begin lifted up through the levels. His ascent starts off slow enough but quickly accelerates up the sixty plus levels. As Sam goes up through the levels he notices that the holes were cut through the floor very recently, and in some places they are still smoldering. Once he arrives at the top another large Theon soldier is there to pull him off the cable and place him on the floor. Fomn is also there, and he gives Sam a curious look before he begins to speak.

"I don't understand why you would put yourself in danger to be here," He says to Sam.

"I have my reasons. How did you get there for me so quickly?"

"My security team wasn't there for you. They were merely securing a possible exit for me if it became necessary. I informed them of your intentions, but we never really thought you'd make it into the building," Fomn says with an amused laugh.

"How did they make it this far into your capitol? I thought you were winning this war. Were you not prepared?" Sam asks.

"We weren't expecting such a poor tactical decision on their part. Currently we are using the attack on the city to tie up enemy soldiers. We have already attacked Bigan and are creating a secured zone there. Our attack will be an important success. I have no idea what the Mirancris expect to get out of this."

"Don't you have weapons that could destroy entire cities?"

"Both sides do. That is why they are not used. It's an unspoken understanding to protect our populations, but since we have the vastly superior fleet it would lead to the extinction of the Mirancris. Still, It has been contemplated, by both sides."

"What's next?"

"We regroup and push back. The Mirancris will regroup, but they will not push. They will leave their slaves to fight and die as the Mirancris and their mercenaries escape. I just don't know what they hoped to achieve from this. It's not like Suphran to make such an erred effort."

"Why is that?" Sam asks curiously.

"Suphran knows they can't beat us by military force. He typically uses much different tactics. Biowarfare, splitting us politically, they even offered us one of the moons around Uncern. That prospect kept us divided for months. Before we declined they attacked, setting us back nearly a year. If not for Suphran this war would have been over long before your arrival. Their use of synthetic slaves in this attack only shows that they need us, and will serve to unify us politically. This does not appear to be a Suphran planned attack. This attack was thought up by someone else."

"If Suphran didn't plan this attack, maybe he suffered the same fate as the Gate's End and the Infinite."

"I don't know, but it is a possibility," Fomn says as he turns to Sam.

"This would make it seem as if the Mirancris are not in control of the vessels."

"I assure you Sam. We do not have the ships, or any Human captives, guests, or envoys, other than yourself of course," Fomn reiterates to Sam.

Back on the Infinite, still in orbit around a distant planet, Suphran is in discussions with his lead intelligence officer, head scientists, and of course his trusted Kiten. At this point his goal is so close he can almost touch it.

"How long till we are ready, and are there any new developments from the interrogations?" Suphran asks.

"The soldiers you asked for are nearly combat ready. They are in the design and numbers you requested. A minimum of ten hours, if we run into complications, twenty-four," Doctor Minger informs him.

Suphran then looks at his intelligence officer and gestures for his answers.

"The live Humans haven't been very cooperative, but never the less we have acquired plenty of intel from them. The vast majority of the Humans are ambassadors, but as expected many were on our list as documented Human intelligence agents."

"So the Humans knowingly put spies on our ship. That is wonderful news," Suphran says with excitement.

"Have you put them on the interrogation device yet?" Suphran asks.

"We started with the Humans on the list of Intelligence agents. I am happy to report we found a plethora of information. Including weapons information, communications information and the location of many Human instillations."

"I'm interested in the instillations. What have we learned? Do we know where they are?"

"There are different stations all around Earth, so many in fact it gives the planet an unnatural silver ring. There are to many to discuss in this meeting, but an individual station list will be in my report. There are also scientific stations or settlements on or orbiting the first four planets and there are instillations of some kind on all the systems moons."

"Military installations, I want to know about them. Have we learned of any A.I. Instillations?"

"The only military instillations we have found are around Earth, and it appears that the machines are still currently completely focused on Venus."

Suphran pauses for a moment. Noticeably disappointed, the genius slowly brings up his hands in anger, but he calms himself and continues his meeting.

"This is not what I want to hear, nor is it what I expected. What you are telling me, is that an intelligent species with a history of war is living next to a tremendous potential threat, yet fear has not forced the creation of military instillations throughout the system. You're missing something," Suphran advises his intelligence officer.

The Intelligence officer puts a hand forward as a polite gesture asking Suphran to wait. Then he begins to discuss some of their other findings.

"The Human brain is substantially different than ours, or even the Theon. When we first put the Humans on the machine we received outrageous results from them. Initial findings showed that these people had extraordinary powers such as flying, the ability to speak with the dead, and living through trauma that their physiology just could not sustain. Several subjects even discovered viscous creatures in storage areas near their primary hibernation platforms."

Suphran laughs long and hard at these findings, then acknowledges a rare error of his own.

"That is my mistake. I should have briefed you. Humans, during there rapid hibernation cycle, endure a strange phenomenon they call a dream. When I first heard of this I was surprised they all hadn't lost their minds, but please go on," Suphran says still laughing at his intel officer's occupational difficulties.

"That information would have assisted me greatly. I almost scrapped the whole program believing they had sabotage their own minds before death. But I must tell you. I did find two of the subjects on our list of spies had the same thoughts about a military instillation."

"And what was this dream," Suphran asks.

"That there is a massive weapons platform hidden in the asteroid belt between the fourth and fifth planets. It may be so secret that the agents didn't have exact locations or even know what it does. All they knew is that it targets the machines. It may have been made as a way to cripple a machine war effort if A.I.'s were to attack Earth. It was very vague, but it is a possibility. As I said, the interrogation device is picking up large amounts of interference from unfiltered parts of the Human mind."

"Can the Humans be resubmitted to the device?"

"They just aren't as sustainable as Theon. We may be able to use the hive cells to keep them alive for a second time in the machine, but it may not be as reliable," The officer tells Suphran.

"Do it and run them again. I also want scouts sent into the belt. If this weapons platform exist I want it located as soon as possible."

Suphran ends the meeting and all the staff, except Kiten, leave the conference room. She then walks to him curiously.

"I assume their will be a large role in this for me," Kiten tells him.

"I need someone I can trust to run the attack portion of what I'm planning. That way I can manage logistics without distraction. As always, you will be my sword Kiten."

Pleased with what she hears, Kiten's face patterns change as she walks out of the conference room.

Left alone in the conference room Suphran returns back to the holographic table, and requests an image of the asteroid belt between Mars and Jupiter. He tries to imagine how he would hide a super weapon in the rocks.

"I know you are out there. Where have they hidden my key?"

Aggressive Deception

Sam listens closely to the chatter Fomn is receiving. In no way does he try to hide his eavesdropping, and in no way does Fomn try to hide the important Theon information he is discussing. Although, Fomn's lack of interest is likely cause Sam's only hearing what he had already predicted. The Mirancris are being pushed back, and their synthetic slave soldiers are being left to fight and die as the Mirancris and their mercenaries escape.

The building they are in has been abandoned by the well trained mercenaries and Mirancris special forces, but the poorly trained synthetics still put on a suicidal show of force fighting Theon rebel forces. Systematically the war ready Theon soldiers kill the enemy synthetics, but they've already served their purpose.

The fighting will go on for a few more hours, and once it ends the Theon will have what they hoped for. They will have a foothold established on the Mirancris world of Bigan, but Mirancris tactics weren't as inept as the Theon leadership believe.

"Sam, you must admit our war does not need your involvement. We are happy for the introduction of our two species, but we did not invite you into this war. The Mirancris invited you into a war they were the catalyst for."

"I'm just an envoy passing information Fomn. Humanity isn't trying to choose sides. We would like to live and learn from both your species, and the Laurine. Peace is our objective," Sam tells Fomn.

"We both know peace is not the only Human objective Sam. Peace is at best a sub-priority. It is even somewhat demeaning that you expect us to believe that it is more," Fomn says clearly annoyed.

Surprised and somewhat bothered by Fomn's tone, Sam looks Fomn in the eye and says what he thinks needs to be said.

"Your honesty is intriguing, but hearing it is disappointing. I'm going to tell you my view of things, and it is far beyond what my superiors would authorize. So remember, this is just one mans opinion. Although I hope the majority of Humanity sees it as I do."

Fomn takes a moment to clear his mind then gestures for Sam to continue.

"Go on. I am looking forward to your opinion as an individual, but I do expect your leaders view to supersede," Fomn says sincerely.

Sam then takes a moment to think about how far he will allow himself to take this discussion. Knowing Van Tellure put him on this assignment for more than just espionage, Sam delves into the experience he had on Venus and works his diplomacy act. Sam speaks clearly and truthfully (as a diplomat should) and let's Fomn know that humanity will voice it's concerns, and the Theon may need to get used to that fact.

"Fomn, if the Theon object to Human and A.I. Involvement, it's for one reason, the planned genocide of the Mirancris. We all know it is wrong, but that is your plan. It can never happen Fomn. I refuse to believe my people will just sit back and allow an entire form of life to be maliciously wiped from existence."

"Is it wrong for a species to advance beyond or defeat their enemies? And you know as well as I that the Mirancris will never accept us as equal. They will eventually develop and spread a pathogen

that will force us into servitude or death. What is
that if not genocide?"

"That's why I'm here, To step away from the
violence and find different, more peaceful
options," Sam says knowing he found a nice place to
end the conversation.

Sam then abandons the discussion and attempts
to get it back on an investigative level. He looks
out the window and sees the city broken, but
moving. He knows from what he has seen that Fomn is
right. The Theon should be free from the constant
specter of biowarfare, but the Mirancris also need
to live. Sam's head aches with the dilemma.

"Fomn, I can't imagine the Mirancris have only
one plan, or one decent strategist to ensure their
future. There is more going on. I don't think this
is a failed invasion effort. What could the
Mirancris possibly have gotten from this attack?"

"We are trying to find out ourselves Sam. Give
us a little time."

Seeing Fomn's annoyance, Sam decides to lay
off the questioning and give the Theon leadership
more time to examine the outcome of the attack.

Onboard the November, Roczi isn't just sitting
around waiting for her next order. She is
monitoring surface combat patterns and space
anomalies. Cloaked ships leave occasional signs of

their presence, and in the space between Bigan and Nictwar their are many. From the over absorption of energy to poor light refraction, there are always signs, and Roczi's not missing a thing.

"Rox, what are you getting from orbit?" Sam asks as he distances himself from Fomn and his soldiers.

"There are only three buildings still under siege, but fighting there is subsiding. There is also still a lot of cloaked movement between the planets Sam. The majority of both fleets are very close, and must be under a very high state of alert."

"You got me worried Rox. We're gunna need the November to get us home."

"We're cloaked and safe. It doesn't appear that the fleets have any desire to attack each other. Both must be focused on more specialized missions."

"I'm not so sure of that. I've seen first hand how these aliens fight. They were meters from each other, positioning and waiting for mistakes. If that's how they fight in spacecraft I don't want you in the crossfire."

"Understood Sam. I'll find somewhere safe."

"Do you have any ideas what the Mirancris could have wanted from such an attack?" Sam asks Roczi.

"My guess would be it's a strategic attack of some kind. Maybe they wanted to cut the head off the snake."

"If that is the case it was still planned poorly. Fomn just doesn't seem to be as big a focus as one would expect. Maybe they were just trying to capture or kill any council members," Sam says to Roczi.

"It's a high price to pay. The Theon now have a foothold on Bigan. But I do have to say the last three buildings seem to be heavily focused on. Talk to Fomn and see what you can find out about them. That's where I would take this."

"Thanks for the advice Rox. Map the buildings and send it to me. I'll see what I can find out."

Sam then walks back to the window and looks out toward the city. He watches the firefights dwindle as the invaders are forced to abandon the planet. He watches till the building maps he requested are received. Then he compares the map to what he sees through the window. Two of the three buildings can be seen along the city's skyline, but the third was to short and obstructed by larger structures. Fomn walks up to Sam and looks out the window with him, also noticing the mapped locations on his communicator.

"I'm impressed with how quickly your information is delivered to you," Fomn tells Sam.

"Those buildings are the last ones showing significant combat."

"I know. Two of those three buildings housed council members, council members that we have been unable to contact or account for. We know what the Mirancris objective was here."

There is a slight pause as Sam tries to put on a display of compassion for the missing council members, but his impatience gets the better of him.

"If you don't mind me asking, what is the significance of the third building?"

There is another slight pause as Fomn lets out a light, cynical laugh at Sam's poor effort in empathy.

"It is a building we thought was a well kept secret. It holds, or held, a pair of Mirancris defectors. They were both members of their military planning division. We were working with them to gain useful intelligence. In return, we would allow them to remain free after their defeat."

"Was any useful information obtained from them?"

"No. It appears Suphran develops and executes his plans very secretively. Even his top officials are mainly just advisors. He comes up with the plans and has few, if any, coordinators. He either has computer assistance, that we cannot locate, or he is somehow able to coordinate their entire defense in his mind."

"Is it possible the defectors were plants?"

"Possible, but unlikely. They were thoroughly searched and had no way of communicating with the Mirancris," Fomn tells Sam, but with noticeable hesitation.

Sam notices the insecurity in Fomn's statement and begins to contemplate the reasons behind. Sam turns his eyes toward the Theon, and is surprised to recognize the expression on his alien face. The Theon council made a crucial mistake trusting the defectors. The uprising has been mostly one sided in the Theon's favor. So much so, that the war seemed to be nearing it's end, but now the Theon may have found themselves fighting a new enemy. One they have created themselves, and the same one that crippled the Mirancris' early efforts to crush the rebellion. The Theon got a taste of arrogance, and complacency soon followed. The extent this error in judgement may cost the rebellion is still unknown.

Frightening Possibilities

Between the Theon held planet of Nictwar and the Mirancris planet of Bigan, two large opposing fleets stalk each other. Neither side will make the first move, so the warships stay cloaked. The fleets have already accomplished their respective short term goals, and now they share a tense unspoken cease fire.

Theon generals had used the Mirancris surprise attack to launch a counter and establish a foothold on Bigan, and the Mirancris had completed their first strategic military attack lead by Commander Kaens in over Two Years. Although the assault seem's to be a failure, Kaens' costly attack was executed exactly as planned.

Suphran's methodically less aggressive tactics were preferred to Kaens more aggressive assaults, but now that Suphran's gone this war has drastically changed.

Preventing massive losses had been the reason for preferring Suphran's tactics, but now the Mirancris' best hope is the brutal genius Commander Kaens. It can be assured, with Kaens now firmly in control, violence and death tolls will increase.

Although the defectors were planted by Suphran merely for information, Kaens decided to use them for a different purpose. The attack on Nictwar was devised to capture Theon council members and interrogate them. Using implanted bio-transmitters, the double agents brought the target information to their new strategist.

On the top floors of the last three buildings under siege Mirancris special forces breach holes leading to the roof tops. On two of the roof tops captured Theon councilmen are taken, and on the third a Mirancris rescue team escorts their double agents. Once the teams arrive with their packages they call for immediate extraction. Small cloaked assault pods quickly fly from one of the capital ships firing at the city. In the aerial assault, the Mirancris spies, rescue teams, and their captured councilmen are able to use cloaks and ascent lines to board waiting extraction ships. The cloaked ships with their precious cargo then leave the planet of Nictwar and quietly ascend to the relative safety of a capital ship.

Once they are onboard the capitol ship the large Mirancris fleet begins to back out of the area. There they will begin the second part of Commander Kaens' plan. In the docking bay all the extraction ships have landed and the occupants are exiting. The two Theon captives are simply escorted to the brig by order of Commander Kaens (who is also in the bay). They Already know, that's where they will sit till they are interrogated and killed.

The new commander is an ambitious military strategist. Unlike Suphran he is a military officer who proudly wears his uniform, but for an officer he is considerably different than one would expect. He prefers a black uniform with black trim and a short black coat that barely reaches his waist. He is considered eccentric (if not mad) by the majority of Mirancris who've met him. Even his chosen coloring is thought to be odd. The commander is clearly taller than Suphran, with nearly white skin and horizontal black pin stripes that significantly widen toward the back. With eyes that resemble the green compound eyes of an Earth insect, Kaens is clearly a different kind of Mirancris. Yet he is still highly respected by his people. His brutal tactics and cruel genius make it necessary.

The two Mirancris spies walk out of their spacecraft, and Kaens is there waiting to greet them.

"Excellent work. The Theon councilmen will likely bring us immensely useful Intel," Kaens tells the two returning spies.

"Thank you commander Kaens. We are happy to assist our people in any way possible."

"I hope your stay on Nictwar was hospitable," Kaens says to them.

"It was. What will be done with the councilmen?" The recently extracted spy asks.

Kaens straitens his stand and looks down at the them disapprovingly. The spy now realizes he said something wrong.

"You have been away for such a long time, and the first question you ask, is about the fate of enemy leadership!" Kaens scolds.

"No commander I was merely..," The spy
says, but Kaens interrupts.

"The fate of the prisoners may scar your
conscious, but they will be taken to an
interrogation device, questioned and tortured
till the device gets all possible information
out of them. If they live through that they
will probably be killed. I haven't decided
yet."

"You will decide?" The other spy asks.

"Yes. If your initial questions were of
our interests, and not that of our enemies, I
would have told you that Suphran is missing.
Now I am in command."

The spy tries to hide his concern for what
he has heard, but the commander sees through
the false confidence.

"What's next for us Commander?" The spy
asks.

"Make your reports then take some leave.
Keep your lives together. Our people will want
to know of all your heroics… The people need
heroes, but mostly they need me. I will turn
the tide of this war."

"Thank you Commander."

With that, the spies leave to fill out their reports and get back to their lives, but Kaens is also paranoid and distrusts them. Even after their bravery and loyalty were displayed during their mission, Kaens is nearly incapable of trusting others. The commander calls over a low ranking officer from another part of the bay, and directs him to quietly monitor the two heroes.

On Nictwar the fighting is done, and the dead lay throughout the streets and pathways of the city. The Theon captured no one, cause none surrendered, and the remaining Theon council members are still trying to find out just what they have lost. The council has only just now chosen a place to meet and discuss the attack. The council needs to determine what they have lost, What they have gained, and what the battle's impact will be. Fomn takes a few aids and begins to leave for the meeting, but Sam objects.

"Fomn I don't see a reason why I shouldn't be allowed to attend this meeting. That is if we are being completely open with each other," Sam say's knowing full well he is already in much deeper than any human government would allow an alien ambassador.

Fomn lets out a small laugh. It's hard to tell, but it seems to have been out of frustration, or possibly amusement.

"Sam, My people have just been attacked. I don't believe you have any right to be a part of this meeting. If anything, you have the right to be expelled!"

"There are many Human ambassadors still unaccounted for. I need to know where they are and who has them."

There is a small pause as Fomn takes in what Sam said. Then he walks up close to Sam (clearly annoyed).

"How do you expect to benefit from this kind behavior Sam?" Fomn says in a whisper.

"I don't want to waste time. The details of this attack are most likely going to be told to me at a later date, and any information obtained could be used to save lives. Maybe, we can even broker an end to this war. Then the fighting can stop, and we can all advance forward."

The room remains quite and Fomn takes Sam to the side.

"In the interest of your noble goals I'll tell you what I already know, and expect. Two council members and the two defectors are not accounted for. They have been captured. I assume they will be interrogated for any information the Mirancris can use."

"I assume the defectors were never fully trusted, so they shouldn't have any useful Intel, and the council members know what's at stake. I doubt they will talk."

"It's true. We never fully trusted the defectors, but the council members have information on ship locations, targets, strategies, and post war plans."

"They will never give up that kind of information. Would they?" Sam asks.

Fomn takes a curious look at Sam, a look that implies he should know.

"They don't have a choice. The Mirancris have devices that extract the answers. They created us. They know more about us then we do."

"The Mirancris can extract answers without cooperation?"

"Of course. They didn't design us to keep secrets," He says to Sam.

"Could this tech be used on Humans?"

"Unlikely, but possible. They are good at what they do. That is all I have for you. Do what you can with that, but I must leave," Fomn tells Sam as he exits the room.

Sam quickly gets ahold of Roczi, and asks for extraction, but he then continues to gripe about having to fill out the reports.

"If you like Sam, I can send them for you," Roczi tells him

"Thank you Roczi, but I'll do these ones myself. See you on the roof."

Minutes later Sam arrives on the roof, where Roczi and the November will soon be for his extraction. Once there, Sam quickly jogs up the ramp.

"Thank you for the quick pick up," Sam tells Roczi.

"Doing your own reports now Sam? That's new for you."

"Yes, I need to send this report with some added information. Then I can forward it to the UNSA. We also need to get back to the Escape. I need to talk to Rizac."

"Whatever you need Sam. Do you believe the Mirancris are capable of modifying their interrogation devices to work on Humans?"

"I don't know, but I want to go over the files from the shuttle and see what kind of information there is on it. I also want to speak with Rizac to see what he may know about it."

Sam is very concerned about this device the Mirancris have, and Roczi can't help but notice.

"Sam, are you alright?"

"I'm fine, just concerned. I know things Rox, information that could put Earth and Venus in immediate jeopardy. And If I was on the Infinite with that information, then so were others with information just as critical," Sam tells Roczi.

"What kind of information Sam? You did say Venus is in jeopardy."

"It's information I can't share with You Roczi."

"Venus is my home, and I deserve the right to save the people I care about, just as you do?" Roczi says to Sam in an urgent tone.

"That's not gunna get it out of me Rox, but I'm putting pieces together and I'm coming up with a pattern. Our system may be in danger, and if so, you'll find out soon enough. Get us to the Escape."

Roczi doesn't waste her time arguing with Sam. Trusting his judgement, Roczi drops the discussion and prepares November for another trip back home. A few moments later, they are back in Earth's system and Roczi is determining their location.

"We are approximately 2 hours away from earth and 2.5 hours away from the Escape."

"Great Rox. Get Zac on the com."

Roczi makes several attempts to contact Zac Van Tellure, but communications are down. Roczi checks the November's communication devices and runs a few scans, but the equipment is all in working order.

"Sam we have a problem. Communications with Earth and Mars are not working. There is something interfering with the com."

"Have we determined the cause?"

"Not yet, but I'm working on it. I should have an answer for you soon. "

"Run more scans, and search for anomalies. Let's see if we can make contact with the Escape, then take us there anyway."

"Right away Sam."

A moment passes, and Roczi runs her scans and attempts to make contact with Rizac on the escape, but there is no answer. The silence is unheard of in the expanding system, and it gives Roczi an ominous feeling.

"There is nothing out there Sam. No answer from Zac or Rizac. I'm not picking up any kind of chatter."

Sam leans forward in his chair and listens intently for any sign of communication from

Roczi's scans, but as intently as he tries, he still hears nothing.

"Net feeds?" Sam asks.

"There is absolutely nothing Sam. It's as if we are in a lifeless system."

"Could it be a solar storm?"

"Unlikely. We would have known it was coming."

Sam closes his eyes and brings his hand to his chin as he contemplates his options. He then stands and walks up next to Roczi at the Helm. With an expressionless face, Sam turns to his closest friend and team member and begins to speak.

"Rox, I may need to clarify my previous involvement with the UNSA. You won't be happy with the details."

I'm All In

Hours later the November arrives at the Escape. Even with the station's highly elliptical orbit communications are barley possible, but they manage to to get ahold of Rizac and begin their approach.

Sam feels very much that something is a miss, and it weighs heavy on his mind. Normally extroverted and talkative, Sam has been quiet since arriving back in the system. The November docks with the station, but as they exit down the November's ramp Roczi can't let Sam's behavior go unquestioned any longer.

"What's going on Sam? I've seen you knowingly and eagerly get yourself into life or death situations. What could possibly have you acting so, un-Sam like?" Roczi asks.

"I may know what's happening, but I'd like to talk to Rizac first and see what he knows about this interrogation device. Can you program one of the warpcoms to go to Earth's customs station and flash S.O.S.?"

"That should be simple. What are we sending?"

"My concerns," Sam tells her as they walk out of the bay and into the Escape's corridors.

Walking quickly through the halls to the bridge, Sam thinks about what he will do if his instincts are correct and this system is under attack. The first thing he needs is information on the Mirancris' interrogation device and the possibility of it being used on Humans.

Sam arrives at the bridge and immediately goes to the main screen.

"Riz, get us visual scans of the entire astroid belt."

"Visual scans? Feeling nostalgic Sam?" Rizac asks.

"No Riz. Just making sure we'll be able to spend all this money we're making."

"Alright Sam. What are we looking for?"

"Any kind of anomalies. Especially those left by cloaked ships."

Rizac complies without further questions and begins his search. In the mean time Sam heads back to his quarters. Once there, Sam will draw up the reports that need to be sent, but Roczi will first meet him on the way.

"I ran the com disruptions through some tests, and I'm pretty sure it's not a natural occurrence," She tells Sam.

"Is there a way to counter it?"

"I'll see if I can come up with something, but I can't promise anything."

"Thank you Rox. That's all I can ask," He tells her.

Sam then continues back to his quarters to fill out the reports. Sam writes his report for the UNSA, but then writes a secondary report for Venetian A.I. Leadership, in case they need to be warned of an attack. Although it only takes a few minutes to fill out his reports, Sam decides he can no longer wait for Roczi to find a way to fix the communication problems.

"Roczi, have you made any progress with communications?" Sam asks over the communicator.

"No. It will take more time to figure out."

"Rizac, any luck on your end," Sam asks.

"Whatever you were thinking Sam, you have it right. There are cloaked ships throughout the astroid belt."

"Are you positive they are ships Riz? I need you to be sure on this."

"I've searched for these types of anomalies the last five years, and these ones were easy to spot."

Sam quickly leaves his quarters for the bridge and approaches Rizac.

"Show me the anomalies you have found?" Sam asks Rizac once he arrives.

Rizac puts the astroid belt on the Main screen and points out what he has found. The anomalies are obvious. Warped light and changes in brightness are clear. Without question, there are cloaked ships in the belt.

"They're moving fast Sam, maybe even recklessly. In fact, I was able to track the anomalies around the the belt. They are moving around the belt at the scan speed of a shuttle. It's like they're searching for something."

Sam takes a step back and puts one hand on his stomach and his other hand on his chin. He then further examines the astroid belt on the screen.

"Please, tell me what you know about the Mirancris' interrogation device. Do you think they could modify it in a way to use it on Humans?" Sam asks closing his eyes and lowering his head, believing he already knows the answer.

"Theon genes are very simple because they have been designed. Mirancris genes are unnecessarily complex. They have been altered by nearly a century of bioengineering. Humans are in a genetic area somewhere in between, but probably easily mapped. I don't think the Mirancris would alter the machine to work on Humans. It's much more likely they would alter the Humans to work with the existing machine."

"So it's possible, and disturbing."

"Yes, very possible."

Sam turns his head and looks at Roczi as she enters the bridge.

"It's the answer you were expecting to hear," Roczi tells him.

"Roczi, send warpcom alpha to the UNSA Station."

"I will. Are you gunna tell us what's going on, or are you going to make us go into our next fight blind?" Roczi asks.

"I'll brief you both before we leave. For now prep for combat, and prepare both the November and the shuttle for departure. Sorry Rizac, but I'm gunna need you to load the remaining 3 droids onto the shuttle and pilot it for this operation."

"Whatever you need Sam, just let me know," Rizac replies.

"Sam, is Venus in danger? Should we warn them?" Roczi asks.

Sam stops to think about what he should do, but then gives Roczi the order anyway.

"Yes. Send warpcom bravo to Venus. I have the information and a warning in it's report."

"What is the warning?" Roczi asks with a look of disbelief.

"Prepare for possible impact."

"What kind of impact Sam?"

"I don't know. I didn't need that information."

After Sam's disclosure, the three prepare for their next mission. Roczi goes to the November and sends off the two warpcoms. One is sent to Earths customs station and the other to Venus, hoping the expected recipients will get the warning. Rizac prepares the shuttle for launch, but Sam is conflicted. The information he knows is from his last mission at the UNSA. Every effort to keep Earths secret weapon quiet has been made. The whole purpose behind Sam's assignment on Venus was to make sure the A.I.s had no idea what the Human governments had designed and put in place in the asteroid belt.

With communications down and no time to warn the UNSA, Sam follows his gut and prays he is right, but at the same time hopes he is wrong. The system is either under attack or he could spend the rest of his life in prison for treason.

Sam draws up a plan then calls his team to the bridge. Roczi enters first and is soon followed by Rizac. Roczi is also the first to speak.

"So Sam, what are we preparing for?"

Sam pauses for a moment, then he takes a breath and begins revealing Humanities biggest secret.

"There is top secret military installation located on 4 Vesta in the asteroid belt. Disguised as a mining operation it's actually a weapon designed to give Humanity an edge if ever attacked by, what was seen at the time to be, Humanities most likely enemy," Sam tells his team.

"What you are saying is there's a giant weapon located in 4 Vesta designed to devastate Venus," Roczi says in an angry tone.

"Yes. I don't fully know of it's capabilities but there is a high probability, from what I've seen, that it is being targeted."

"Why do you think the Mirancris would attack a Human installation? What could they possibly gain?" Rizac asks curiously.

"I have some ideas, but I don't know for sure."

"If the the Mirancris are desperate enough they may want any intervention. If we A.I.s feel threatened, we may force the warring factions into talks. Especially if the war overflows into our system," Roczi adds.

"Neither side is acknowledging holding the envoys, but if the Mirancris have managed to use the interrogation device on Humans the instillation may be compromised," Sam Says.

"The reasoning for it can be discussed later. We need to get over there. Hopefully we have the weapons to hold off attackers till help can arrive," Roczi says.

"Com transmissions are being jammed somehow, so we'll need to keep optical sensors open for code. That's how we'll coordinate once we are there. We'll stay cloaked and land on the astroid, hopefully unnoticed or at least unopposed. I have no idea how to get in the instillation, so our options are to try and scan for an entrance, which will likely be masked, or we may have to place an explosive on the surface and see if we can find an entrance using ground penetrating sonar. Any ideas?" Sam asks.

"We can skip the scans. It's a waste of time," Roczi tells Sam.

"I can stay cloaked in orbit and use a hand held grenade launcher as the explosive charge. It will mark our arrival, but our exact location should still be concealed," Rizac offers.

"It's a good idea Rizac. It should also put the soldiers inside on alert if they aren't already," Roczi adds.

"Hopefully none of that will need to be done. I may be able to just land, knock on the door, and let them know of our concerns. Lets suit up, get moving, and hope for the best, cause this plan of ours is full of problems," Sam tells his crew in a way that fails to inspire hope, but does get a bit of a chuckle from Rizac.

"We can't risk doing nothing. We have to see for ourselves, and possibly try to stop it," Roczi tells Sam with a look of concern.

The three go to the ships. Sam and Roczi to the November and Rizac to the shuttle. Each ship armed with combat droids and gun pods that Sam once expected to sell to aspiring space pirates, but now they may be used to prevent the taking of Earth's super weapon, and stop millions, if not billions of deaths.

The voyage to 4 Vesta is about five hours, so Sam begins his pre-mission ritual shortly after leaving the Escape. Sitting in his captains chair he puts his feet up, leans back and let's his mind drift. Four hours later Roczi begins her ritual of waking Sam, asking him how he can sleep at a time like this, and getting him ready, but this time Roczi has her own surprises for Sam.

"Sam, we're about an hour away from 4 Vesta. You should get up, gear up and get ready."

"Right as always Rox. I have to tell you, I feel very uncertain about this."

"This one is different Sam. We are completely clueless as to what we are heading into. We could be heading into a tightly held and heavily occupied planetoid of death. If that's the case, you may be hailed a hero, or you could have just given up Humanity's most secret weapon. which if that is the case you will be tried for treason."

"There is a lot of possibilities between your two extremes Rox."

"No there's not, but you should know what an unselfish and brave act you are performing. You could do nothing or just run off to Mars Station and come out a hero just for the effort you have already put in. Instead, you decide to risk it all to stop it. I see right through your shallow facade Sam, or should I say your facade of shallow," Roczi says as she walks up closer to Sam.

"What? Never mind. We gotta go," Sam replies with a confused look.

Sam walks off the bridge heading to his quarters, but before leaving he makes one last remark.

"Rox, you know if I am wrong about this, I don't plan on standing trial," Sam says just as he leaves the room.

Back in his quarters Sam puts on his usual grey and black ensemble, but this time there's a heated thermal space suit that goes over it all, with a helmet and oxygen regenerator. Sam makes his way to the armory where he will leave most of his usual pistols behind for larger more powerful weapons. Sam picks up a fully automatic, armor piercing battle rifle, a magnetic armor piercing submachine gun, and extra ammunition. Sam then grabs a bunch of grenades and is about to walk out when he sees the peijax Rizac made for him. Remembering how useful it was on Nictwar he takes it too.

Sam arrives at the bridge and is surprised by what he sees. Roczi is in full combat gear, complete with a magnetic submachine gun and hand held grenade launcher.

"What are you all dressed up for?" Sam asks smiling.

"I'm going with you."

"Who's going to give me real time scans from the ship?"

"Whatever is being used to jam the coms may keep us from communicating, even through the short distance. I'm not letting you go in blind."

"Are you programmed for combat?"

"I downloaded recon and combat programs a year ago, just incase I ever needed to get you out of a mess. I'm more qualified for this than you are."

"How do you plan on communicating with me on the surface?"

"Through the translator. It will work. Trust me."

"Alright Rox. Find a crater and set us down in it's shadow. I'm happy you're coming with me on this one," Sam tells her.

"Thank you Sam. I'm happy to go with you, but It's even nicer knowing we have three walking tanks coming with us."

Sam smiles and nods his head in agreement.

"Lets get started," He says.

On approach, 4 Vesta looks normal. Only craters and mining equipment are running on its airless surface, but looks can be deceiving. At a minimum, there is at least one cloaked ship with three combat droids currently descending into one of her craters, and one larger but equally armed cloaked vessel in orbit around the astroid.

The November slowly sets down. Roczi and Sam are now ready to begin their assault on a super weapon.

Into The Fire

Hours later the November arrives at the Escape. Even with the station's highly elliptical orbit communications are barley possible, but they manage to to get ahold of Rizac and begin their approach.

Sam feels very much that something is a miss, and it weighs heavy on his mind. Normally extroverted and talkative, Sam has been quiet since arriving back in the system. The November docks with the station, but as they exit down the November's ramp Roczi can't let Sam's behavior go unquestioned any longer.

"What's going on Sam? I've seen you knowingly and eagerly get yourself into life or death situations. What could possibly have you acting so, un-Sam like?" Roczi asks.

"I may know what's happening, but I'd like to talk to Rizac first and see what he knows about this interrogation device. Can you program one of the warpcoms to go to Earth's customs station and flash S.O.S.?"

"That should be simple. What are we sending?"

"My concerns," Sam tells her as they walk out of the bay and into the Escape's corridors.

Walking quickly through the halls to the bridge, Sam thinks about what he will do if his instincts are correct and this system is under attack. The first thing he needs is information on the Mirancris' interrogation device and the possibility of it being used on Humans.

Sam arrives at the bridge and immediately goes to the main screen.

"Riz, get us visual scans of the entire astroid belt."

"Visual scans? Feeling nostalgic Sam?" Rizac asks.

"No Riz. Just making sure we'll be able to spend all this money we're making."

"Alright Sam. What are we looking for?"

"Any kind of anomalies. Especially those left by cloaked ships."

Rizac complies without further questions and begins his search. In the mean time Sam heads back to his quarters. Once there, Sam will draw up the reports that need to be sent, but Roczi will first meet him on the way.

"I ran the com disruptions through some tests, and I'm pretty sure it's not a natural occurrence," She tells Sam.

"Is there a way to counter it?"

"I'll see if I can come up with something, but I can't promise anything."

"Thank you Rox. That's all I can ask," He tells her.

Sam then continues back to his quarters to fill out the reports. Sam writes his report for the UNSA, but then writes a secondary report for Venetian A.I. Leadership, in case they need to be warned of an attack. Although it only takes a few minutes to fill out his reports, Sam decides he can no longer wait for Roczi to find a way to fix the communication problems.

"Roczi, have you made any progress with communications?" Sam asks over the communicator.

"No. It will take more time to figure out."

"Rizac, any luck on your end," Sam asks.

"Whatever you were thinking Sam, you have it
right. There are cloaked ships throughout the
astroid belt."

"Are you positive they are ships Riz? I need
you to be sure on this."

"I've searched for these types of anomalies
the last five years, and these ones were easy to
spot."

Sam quickly leaves his quarters for the bridge
and approaches Rizac.

"Show me the anomalies you have found?" Sam
asks Rizac once he arrives.

Rizac puts the astroid belt on the Main screen
and points out what he has found. The anomalies are
obvious. Warped light and changes in brightness are
clear. Without question, there are cloaked ships in
the belt.

"They're moving fast Sam, maybe even
recklessly. In fact, I was able to track the
anomalies around the the belt. They are moving
around the belt at the scan speed of a shuttle.
It's like they're searching for something."

Sam takes a step back and puts one hand on his
stomach and his other hand on his chin. He then
further examines the astroid belt on the screen.

"Please, tell me what you know about the Mirancris' interrogation device. Do you think they could modify it in a way to use it on Humans?" Sam asks closing his eyes and lowering his head, believing he already knows the answer.

"Theon genes are very simple because they have been designed. Mirancris genes are unnecessarily complex. They have been altered by nearly a century of bioengineering. Humans are in a genetic area somewhere in between, but probably easily mapped. I don't think the Mirancris would alter the machine to work on Humans. It's much more likely they would alter the Humans to work with the existing machine."

"So it's possible, and disturbing."

"Yes, very possible."

Sam turns his head and looks at Roczi as she enters the bridge.

"It's the answer you were expecting to hear," Roczi tells him.

"Roczi, send warpcom alpha to the UNSA Station."

"I will. Are you gunna tell us what's going on, or are you going to make us go into our next fight blind?" Roczi asks.

"I'll brief you both before we leave. For now prep for combat, and prepare both the November and the shuttle for departure. Sorry Rizac, but I'm gunna need you to load the remaining 3 droids onto the shuttle and pilot it for this operation."

"Whatever you need Sam, just let me know," Rizac replies.

"Sam, is Venus in danger? Should we warn them?" Roczi asks.

Sam stops to think about what he should do, but then gives Roczi the order anyway.

"Yes. Send warpcom bravo to Venus. I have the information and a warning in it's report."

"What is the warning?" Roczi asks with a look of disbelief.

"Prepare for possible impact."

"What kind of impact Sam?"

"I don't know. I didn't need that information."

After Sam's disclosure, the three prepare for their next mission. Roczi goes to the November and sends off the two warpcoms. One is sent to Earths customs station and the other to Venus, hoping the expected recipients will get the warning. Rizac

prepares the shuttle for launch, but Sam is
conflicted. The information he knows is from his
last mission at the UNSA. Every effort to keep
Earths secret weapon quiet has been made. The whole
purpose behind Sam's assignment on Venus was to
make sure the A.I.s had no idea what the Human
governments had designed and put in place in the
asteroid belt.

With communications down and no time to warn
the UNSA, Sam follows his gut and prays he is
right, but at the same time hopes he is wrong. The
system is either under attack or he could spend the
rest of his life in prison for treason.

Sam draws up a plan then calls his team to the
bridge. Roczi enters first and is soon followed by
Rizac. Roczi is also the first to speak.

"So Sam, what are we preparing for?"

Sam pauses for a moment, then he takes a
breath and begins revealing Humanities biggest
secret.

"There is top secret military installation
located on 4 Vesta in the asteroid belt. Disguised
as a mining operation it's actually a weapon
designed to give Humanity an edge if ever attacked
by, what was seen at the time to be, Humanities
most likely enemy," Sam tells his team.

"What you are saying is there's a giant weapon located in 4 Vesta designed to devastate Venus," Roczi says in an angry tone.

"Yes. I don't fully know of it's capabilities but there is a high probability, from what I've seen, that it is being targeted."

"Why do you think the Mirancris would attack a Human installation? What could they possibly gain?" Rizac asks curiously.

"I have some ideas, but I don't know for sure."

"If the the Mirancris are desperate enough they may want any intervention. If we A.I.s feel threatened, we may force the warring factions into talks. Especially if the war overflows into our system," Roczi adds.

"Neither side is acknowledging holding the envoys, but if the Mirancris have managed to use the interrogation device on Humans the instillation may be compromised," Sam Says.

"The reasoning for it can be discussed later. We need to get over there. Hopefully we have the weapons to hold off attackers till help can arrive," Roczi says.

"Com transmissions are being jammed somehow, so we'll need to keep optical sensors open for

code. That's how we'll coordinate once we are
there. We'll stay cloaked and land on the astroid,
hopefully unnoticed or at least unopposed. I have
no idea how to get in the instillation, so our
options are to try and scan for an entrance, which
will likely be masked, or we may have to place an
explosive on the surface and see if we can find an
entrance using ground penetrating sonar. Any
ideas?" Sam asks.

"We can skip the scans. It's a waste of time,"
Roczi tells Sam.

"I can stay cloaked in orbit and use a hand
held grenade launcher as the explosive charge. It
will mark our arrival, but our exact location
should still be concealed," Rizac offers.

"It's a good idea Rizac. It should also put
the soldiers inside on alert if they aren't
already," Roczi adds.

"Hopefully none of that will need to be done.
I may be able to just land, knock on the door, and
let them know of our concerns. Lets suit up, get
moving, and hope for the best, cause this plan of
ours is full of problems," Sam tells his crew in a
way that fails to inspire hope, but does get a bit
of a chuckle from Rizac.

"We can't risk doing nothing. We have to see
for ourselves, and possibly try to stop it," Roczi
tells Sam with a look of concern.

The three go to the ships. Sam and Roczi to the November and Rizac to the shuttle. Each ship armed with combat droids and gun pods that Sam once expected to sell to aspiring space pirates, but now they may be used to prevent the taking of Earth's super weapon, and stop millions, if not billions of deaths.

The voyage to 4 Vesta is about five hours, so Sam begins his pre-mission ritual shortly after leaving the Escape. Sitting in his captains chair he puts his feet up, leans back and let's his mind drift. Four hours later Roczi begins her ritual of waking Sam, asking him how he can sleep at a time like this, and getting him ready, but this time Roczi has her own surprises for Sam.

"Sam, we're about an hour away from 4 Vesta. You should get up, gear up and get ready."

"Right as always Rox. I have to tell you, I feel very uncertain about this."

"This one is different Sam. We are completely clueless as to what we are heading into. We could be heading into a tightly held and heavily occupied planetoid of death. If that's the case, you may be hailed a hero, or you could have just given up Humanity's most secret weapon. which if that is the case you will be tried for treason."

"There is a lot of possibilities between your two extremes Rox."

"No there's not, but you should know what an unselfish and brave act you are performing. You could do nothing or just run off to Mars Station and come out a hero just for the effort you have already put in. Instead, you decide to risk it all to stop it. I see right through your shallow facade Sam, or should I say your facade of shallow," Roczi says as she walks up closer to Sam.

"What? Never mind. We gotta go," Sam replies with a confused look.

Sam walks off the bridge heading to his quarters, but before leaving he makes one last remark.

"Rox, you know if I am wrong about this, I don't plan on standing trial," Sam says just as he leaves the room.

Back in his quarters Sam puts on his usual grey and black ensemble, but this time there's a heated thermal space suit that goes over it all, with a helmet and oxygen regenerator. Sam makes his way to the armory where he will leave most of his usual pistols behind for larger more powerful weapons. Sam picks up a fully automatic, armor piercing battle rifle, a magnetic armor piercing submachine gun, and extra ammunition. Sam then grabs a bunch of grenades and is about to walk out when he sees the peijax Rizac made for him. Remembering how useful it was on Nictwar he takes it too.

216

Sam arrives at the bridge and is surprised by what he sees. Roczi is in full combat gear, complete with a magnetic submachine gun and hand held grenade launcher.

"What are you all dressed up for?" Sam asks smiling.

"I'm going with you."

"Who's going to give me real time scans from the ship?"

"Whatever is being used to jam the coms may keep us from communicating, even through the short distance. I'm not letting you go in blind."

"Are you programmed for combat?"

"I downloaded recon and combat programs a year ago, just incase I ever needed to get you out of a mess. I'm more qualified for this than you are."

"How do you plan on communicating with me on the surface?"

"Through the translator. It will work. Trust me."

"Alright Rox. Find a crater and set us down in it's shadow. I'm happy you're coming with me on this one," Sam tells her.

"Thank you Sam. I'm happy to go with you, but It's even nicer knowing we have three walking tanks coming with us."

Sam smiles and nods his head in agreement.

"Lets get started," He says.

On approach, 4 Vesta looks normal. Only craters and mining equipment are running on its airless surface, but looks can be deceiving. At a minimum, there is at least one cloaked ship with three combat droids currently descending into one of her craters, and one larger but equally armed cloaked vessel in orbit around the astroid.

The November slowly sets down. Roczi and Sam are now ready to begin their assault on a super weapon.

Misfit
Fleet

Onboard an alien shuttle Kiten and Nico Watch as 4 Vesta and it's hidden weapons platform are retaken by Earths military forces. As expected, the reinforcements Suphran sent fought to the death, and we're even seen killing a few Laurine mercenaries trying to escape with their lives. Kiten sees enough, and her appetite for the truth has been filled. The shuttle slowly drifts further away from the astroid belt with her cloak engaged.

"You failed to take the station, and you should have had the upper hand. What do you think happened?" Nico asks Kiten.

"I think the outcome was planned. Supposed to look like a Theon attack I assume."

"You must have thought it was a possibility. Otherwise I wouldn't be here."

"Yes, I anticipated this. I just needed to be sure. Take us to the Infinite. Keep us cloaked," Kiten orders.

Nico takes the shuttle away from the belt and warps them back to the infinite, but at a vast distance where they won't be noticed. After they arrive, it still takes hours to get near the Infinite's location. This gives Kiten added time to come up with ideas.

"The Infinite and the Gate's End are in sight. Do you want us to hail," Nico asks.

"Negative. Keep scanning for departing shuttles. If I'm right, Suphran will not allow himself to be in exile, but he cannot allow the loss of all the valuable data the scientists have obtained. He will return to a Mirancris outpost to plead his case and speak of his heroic deeds. I'm sure there will be more to it. After all, it is one of Suphran's plans."

"I'm picking up a shuttle leaving the infinite," Niko advises.

"That would be Suphran. After the ship jumps take us to the vessel."

Suphran's shuttle jumps shortly there after and Nico takes the shuttle to the infinite, but there are no bay lights or doors opening for them.

Kiten tries to reach the ship by communicator but there is no response.

"Suphran has the coms down. That is not good news for the ships," Kiten tells Nico.

"It appears the ships aren't leaving orbit."

"Suphran will want to destroy the evidence."

"Shouldn't he just blow up the ships?"

"He must not be finished with them, but we don't have much time."

"We Must wait for another ship to come back or leave, so we can slip in. That will be tricky," Nico tells Kiten.

"No. We need someone with enough knowledge to get us past the ships systems. A high ranking military officer who would be willing to help us."

"We may have to abandon your plan for the ships," Nico tells Kiten.

"No. Suphran will want someone to take the fall for the attack on the Human base."

There is a short pause, then Kiten looks at the helm.

"I know where to get our high ranking officer," Kiten continues.

"Good, cause my ideas are much bigger than this shuttle," Nico says.

"Our opportunity has arrived, and I refuse to let it slip through my fingers. Take us to the Bigan-Nictwar front. That's where we'll find our officer.

A shuttle arrives in the Bigan-Nictwar system. The ship is cloaked and hours away from the two worlds. Onboard Suphran is confident of his plan and purpose. Steadfast in his efforts, a message is sent from the shuttle.

It states "I am safe, and catastrophe has been averted. I need to be heard to save my people from further deception and destruction. I need assistance."

Suphran waits nearly ten minutes and nothing is received. Finally, a response reaches the shuttle.

"Please announce yourself and state your service."

Suphran steps away from the communicator to think about what he may have omitted from his message. He momentarily laughs at what he has left out, and adds to his previous message.

"I am Suphran, and I am requesting aid. Please give me instruction."

Minutes pass as Suphran imagines the Mirancris onboard the ships celebrating as news of his return spreads. His thoughts are correct. Even before his arrival was confirmed rumors he would return as their strategic commander had been spread by hopeful Mirancris. The chatter is inspiring, and the inspiration is allowed and encouraged by the Mirancris leadership. It is encouraged so much that the capitol ships back further away from the confrontation area just so the news can spread through unfiltered, and unencrypted channels. The Mirancris clearly want the news to spread, but the uninhibited communications leave the capitol ships detectable. Now, someone just entering the system picks up the chatter from the Mirancris vessels. Kiten and Nico have arrived with their sensors wide open.

Kiten enters the system and hears the hoopla throughout the system on Mirancris channels. She is stunned by the audacity of the Mirancris chatter.

"They're acting as if they won the war," Kiten tells Nico in disbelief.

"It does makes it real easy to locate a capitol ship with this amount of com traffic. Would you like us to go there?"

"That's where our target is."

Nico turns and looks at Kiten.

"Tell me we're not going after Suphran. We would never make it out of the system," Nico says to her.

"No. We're going after his target. He may fight for now, but he will thank us later."

"Kiten, Who is our target?"

"Commander Kaens. I believe Suphran has set him up for a fall. One that he is not prepared for."

"And you believe he will help us obtain the Gate's End and the Infinite?"

"We'll let him know what his options are. He will quickly understand that coming with us is his only viable option."

"What if he doesn't comply?" Niko asks.

"We take him anyway. Then we just hope he comes to terms with his new role."

"It's our best shot at getting what we want."

"And what is it you want?" Kiten asks.

"I don't know, but it's more than this."

Kiten and Nico are in agreement. The risk is worth it, even if it's only revenge their after.

"Take us in Nico. We will take the Commander, and with him we take the ships."

Kiten's shuttle closes in on the capitol ship. They approach the large vessel where they see Suphran's luxury shuttle uncloak, and giant bay doors open awaiting Suphran's shuttle.

"Let's move! Open the bay door. We'll use the cable," Kiten orders.

This may be Kiten and Nico's only chance to get onboard, and they know it. The shuttle door opens and Nico launches the cable to its limit, barely reaching the bay door. Niko and Kiten abandon their shuttle and use the magnetic cable to pull themselves to the capitol ship. From there the two quietly slip into the shuttle bay and wait for their moment.

Suphran's spacecraft then enters the shuttle bay. The atmosphere field glows slightly as it enters. Then the shuttle lands and the ships bay doors close. Soon the ships captan also enters the bay with commander Kaens and several security officers. Suphran exits the shuttle. As he walks down the ramp his expression is that of exhaustion, but he appears angry at the site of Kaens.

"Captain! Have Kaens taken into custody!" Suphran shouts.

No action is immediately taken, but then Suphran begins announcing charges.

"He is charged with interfering with diplomatic missions, and unauthorized acts of war bordering on treason. Captain arrest him as I am still searching for his coconspirators," Suphran clearly says as a threat.

"Do you have evidence of this?" The Captain asks.

"It is all right here in these logs. He was going to place responsibility for it on me," Suphran tells the captain as he hands him a data pad.

"These charges are insane! Suphran, what is the purpose of this?" Kaens questions, but he gets no answer.

Soon, the confused captain orders his officers to take Kaens into custody, but Fuming with anger and confused, Kaens is not one to just accept this fate.

"I will get out, and I will remember this. My redemption will be your disgrace," He tells Suphran.

Kaens then leaves with his escorts cooperatively. Waiting for his chance to speak in court.

"Captain, will you take me to your com center? I need to get in touch with the Vycelar. They need to be updated on Commander Kaens' activities in the Earth System," Suphran tells the Captain.

The Captain quickly leads Suphran out of the bay and to the communication center.

"We have to act now," Kiten advises Niko as she runs out of hiding and toward the door.

Niko follows, but he is less familiar with the Mirancris architecture. Kaens isn't far, but once beyond the bay doors they have to proceed with caution not to be noticed in cloak. They find Kaens being escorted by only two soldiers. Kiten and Niko act without hesitation.

The Laurine and modified Human use their advanced combat training in a well timed and coordinated attack. Both take out their blades and approach the security officers from behind, then swiftly and quietly slice their throats. Kaens simply turns, and watches his escorts die.

"Who are you, and what is this new twist?" Kaens asks in an entirely calm manner.

"You're being set up. You may stay here and
hope Suphran, a person who has been called the
savior, fails to persuade others into believing
you're guilt. Or you can come with us, and start a
new life with two capitol ships and lead hundreds,
and soon thousands. Time is short, so choose
quickly," Kiten tells Kaens.

Kaens doesn't have to think long about his
situation. He begins walking back to the docking
bays before Kiten even finishes her pitch.

"I've heard enough. We'll take my shuttle but
we need to move quickly before it's secured," Kaens
tells his new partners.

Just as planned, the three abandoned join
together and take Kaens' shuttle out of the capitol
ship. Kiten's swiftly executed plan ensures that
Kaens' clearances are not revoked in time to
prevent their escape. They leave the capital ship
onboard Kaens' shuttle and quickly warp back to the
location of the their future fleet.

The three arrive at the distant system with
the Infinite and Gate's End in view. Kaens is
clearly impressed with what he sees, and he lets it
be known.

"This is wonderful! Two capitol ships with
fighters and shuttles. This is an excellent
opportunity!" Kaens enthusiastically states.

"If you get us in, they are ours," Niko says.

"I can get you in, but you have to take care of any resistance inside."

"There will be no resistance. They still believe they're working for the military," Kiten tells him.

"Sounds like an excellent career move. I far prefer this to imprisonment," Kaens confidently tells his new partners.

The Results are In

Sam requested to have his debriefing with Zac Van Tellure at the same Mars space station they had met before, in the same lounge, with the same bartender, and the sam drinks. Sam tends to his tequila and Zac with his bourbon. With the mission over the mood very light, and a stiff tension has been lifted.

The two men sit in the bar sipping their drinks, discussing their thoughts on the outcome of the operations without bringing up the details. The details will come up later on, when the men have had enough to drink, and don't mind reliving the missions. There will probably be a little embellishment added to their stories as well.

"Zac, you must have looked pretty good during this whole thing. What lies ahead for you?"

"There is still a lot of work to do. Because of the way things turned out, the Mirancris are not as fourth coming as we would have wanted. It appears no species likes being told to cease and desist their warring activities. That persists even if it saves their species from annihilation. The Theon turned out to be more of a problem than expected as well. If not for Venusian involvement, I believe they would have continued the war."

"What of the A.I.'s? Do they have any idea of how close they came to the end of their bliss in subterranean Venus?" Sam asks.

"We don't know what they know, but they know something. They have began recruiting for a military, and they have been seen searching the system. That base on 4 Vesta, it's purpose needs to be changed," Zac tells Sam shaking his head.

"What about you Sam?"

"Me?"

"Yes. You were without question the biggest part of this entire mission. You have been key to my rise within the UNSA. You acquired all the information requested, advancing Humanity by half a century, if not more. You saved a military base, and possibly saved one of our inner planets from a devastating attack. Not to mention, you played a big part in ending a war that was leading to the extinction of an intelligent species," Van Tellure says to Sam.

"I'm not taking credit for ending this war.
Our intervention was brought on by circumstances we
may never be sure of. We don't know for certain who
attacked the base, or what their reasons were. For
all we know we facilitated the attackers
objective."

"Even if that is the case, all our objectives
have been met. If nothing else you may have
prevented us from becoming part of this war. After
the inquiries are made, results are determined and
medals are given ,Yours and mine will be given in
private, of course, You will have to accept the
part you played in this."

Then the pretty brunette bartender Jessica
comes by with another round of drinks.

"You two look like you will be needing a few
more of these. Should I start a tab?" She asks with
a smile on her face.

"No thank you. We're almost finished here, but
would you put some baseball on the screen for us
please? Thank you," Zac answers quickly.

Jessica leaves the table dropping off a few
drinks and turns on the screen. On it appears a
baseball game, but the players seem slow and
lethargic.

"Alright! We get to see real people playing the game. This may be a little slower paced than we've been used to," Zac says.

"I want something a little slower paced after what we've been through."

"There is something I want to ask you Sam, do you have any desire to come back to the agency? There won't always be a need for your services otherwise, and we really want to keep you as part of this."

Sam thinks for a moment. Then he takes another sip, and slowly brings his gaze back to Jessica.

"I tried sticking with it before Zac. I was only disappointed by the assignments I received after my service on Venus. I prefer my role now," Sam answers.

"I'll get you back in the field, and we're still trying to figure out who coordinated the attack. People are missing, the Theon and Mirancris both deny any knowledge or involvement, and the Mirancris are mildly pushing the possibility of a rouge faction from either side. After all, there are still two missing capitol ships whose whereabouts are completely unknown. There is plenty the agency, and Humanity can use from you right now Sam."

"Obtaining information does seem to be a strong point of mine, and finding out what happened to the capitol ships is intriguing, but I won't do it as an employee of the agency. Under contract would be a different story though," Sam tells Zac hoping for a third contract to search for the missing envoys.

"Patience Sam. We're prioritizing assignments and we may call on you, just not yet."

Sam stands up and finishes his drink.

"I'll be waiting for the call. You want me in cause I get the job done. I also happen to bring a few extras to the table," Sam tells him.

Then Zac stands and finishes his drink.

"We'll see Sam. Until then stay sharp. I would say try to relax, but you don't seem to have any trouble with that."

"We'll talk soon," Sam says as Zac shakes his hand and walks out of the bar.

The lounge is now almost completely empty, with the exception of Sam and the bartender, Jessica. Sam did request to have this meeting at this station for a reason. Jessica has been in his head since the last time he seen her, but Sam doesn't like to take on to many assignments at once.

Sam is a confident one, and as he approaches the brunette behind the bar he gets Roczi on the communicator.

"Roczi, I'm hoping to be late. Please be patient. I'll let you know how things go when I get back."

"Gotcha Sam. I'll be tending to the ship till you return. Enjoy yourself Sam. You deserve it."

Roczi is on the November waiting in her quarters when she gets the message from Sam, but right after the message Roczi leaves her quarters and enters the cargo bay. She finds herself a warpcom and begins to record a message.

"Venusian Intelligence, This is agent K-68-DC Roczi. It's been over two years but the suspicions of a Human military platform have been confirmed. The mining operation on 4 Vesta is a cover for some type of super weapon. There was an attempt from an alien species to take the weapon but earth forces retained the base. My mission is complete, and I am leaving Venusian Intelligence at this time. If you have any further questions, I will stay in the employment of Sam Stix. End of report."

Roczi opens the November's cargo bay door and launches the Warpcom to her former superiors on Venus. With her planet a little safer and her long time mission complete, Roczi leaves her employment with the Venusian Special Objectives Division to continue working with Sam.

She too is confident. Confident she can do more for the safety of the system with Sam.

What's Next

Roczi walks throughout the November. Its
corridors dim as she passes by. Appreciating the
beautiful surroundings, she smiles as she walks.
She makes her way into the armory, where she begins
cleaning weapons. When she's done with that she
begins testing sensors and communications
connections.

Roczi is just keeping herself busy since the
end of the UNSA contract, but she still doesn't yet
feel as if the mission is finished. The two missing
ships and unaccounted for Humans haunt her. It
haunts her just as much as it does Sam. Their
missions may have been a success, but as far as
Roczi and Sam are concerned it is not complete.

The sound of a mechanical door shutting
abruptly stops her from her menial tasks. Roczi
puts down the sensor embedded suit she was working
on and grabs one of the pistols she just cleaned.
She then tactically leaves the armory. Using her
sensors she finds the intruder on the bridge. The
intruder is Human, a fact that relaxes her before
she even gets there. She opens the door and sees
Sam laying way back in his captains chair. Putting

her gun away she walks up to Sam and sits on the control panel in front of him.

"How did things go?" Roczi asks as she crosses her legs.

"They went well, although not as well as I hoped. As you can see, I'm back much earlier than expected."

"I'm surprised you didn't notify me you were coming back."

"It slipped my mind."

"Speaking of your mind, something appears to be on it," Roczi says with curiosity.

"I figured I couldn't hide it from you."

"What is it Sam? Are you concerned about the missing people?"

"Course I am Rox, but that's not it."

Roczi then leans in toward Sam, and he looks back at her.

"We have worked together closely for the past two years Sam. You should feel a little more open to talk to me."

"It's really just not that important Rox."

Roczi now leans back slightly and cocks her head to one side as a dismayed look comes across her face.

"What is important to you Sam? In the time I've known you, I have watched you form relationships with people just to neglect them and see them wither away. I know you worked for the UNSA, but you weren't happy there. I've been with you as you earned a fortune in the black, white, and grey markets, but the whole time you never seemed content. Tell me what makes you happy Sam. That is, if you even know."

Sam's eyes widen as Roczi talks. There is a brief silence, but then Sam smiles.

"Wow Roczi! That is truly what I'm thinking about, in a way."

"What do you mean "in a way"?"

"I know my life has been much more eventful than most others, and I may be successful, but I just feel empty. There is something missing Rox."

"What are you thinking Sam? Do you think it may be time to hang it up? Take your earnings back to earth and find another occupation, or start a family?"

"I don't know Rox. I haven't really thought about it until now. Maybe I'm just a little spent

239

from the last mission, or maybe having the little bit of normal Human interaction tonight reminded me that there is more out there. The one thing I'm certain about, is that I shouldn't need life advice from a five year old machine whom is supposed to be learning from me."

"That is pretty sad Sam."

The two share a brief laugh at the irony, and enjoy the moment.

"I'm a horrible example for a young A.I.," Sam says with a smile on his face.

"I should have never taken this position, but it was the best decision I've ever made," She says.

"Thank you Rox. I couldn't have made it this far without you."

"You're welcome. Now I suggest you get some rest, and in the morning I'll take you down to the Martian surface. There we will find a few fun things to clear your head. I know the stress of what you've been through can be very disruptive to the Human body."

"I like your idea, and I wouldn't want to make any rash life decisions," Sam says as he pushes himself out of his captains chair and starts walking back to his quarters.

Roczi tells Sam goodnight as he walks away. In
return, Sam merely gives her a little wave and some
inaudible remark. Sam is clearly spent, but Roczi
enjoyed her little talk with him. It is the first
time she has seen such a Human side of Sam. She
smiles as she thinks about it. Then she hops off
the control panel and decides to call it a night
herself, but in her case this only means she will
retire to her quarters and run some self
diagnostics and reconditioning programs. She has
earned herself a night of rest as well.

The next morning Roczi drags Sam to the
Martian surface. She tells him it will be good for
his soul to get out and get a little better
acquainted to normal society. Even if it is just a
high glass dome settlement. Sam objects at first,
wanting to go back to the escape, but Sam can't
disagree with Roczi's logic. Besides that, Sam
feels he hasn't been helping her learn about Human
interaction, and he feels as if he may be slipping
in that aspect as well.

Over the last few years the vast majority of
his time has been spent alone, with Roczi, or with
business acquaintances. Half of those acquaintances
would be considered undesirable in the first place.
People such as the Saunders, who acted like his
friends but then tried to kill him to avoid paying

for his services. The worst thing about it is how
he recognized the changes happening within himself
and just allowed it to happen. After all, he did
get into the Saunders deal full knowing that things
may go wrong and he may have to kill them.

The first place Roczi takes Sam is out clothes
shopping. Although his clothes have been well kept
it had been a while since he bought anything new,
and even his machine counterpart wants him to bring
some color into his black and grey wardrobe. It
will not go so well for Roczi. Most of what she
suggests is shot down, but she does get him to buy
some dark earth and dark rust colored items. He
also changes it up a bit by buying some rimmed
hats. Those too are black, grey, and dark earth
colored. Still, Sam puts on a dark earth colored
coat and hat for Roczi.

As they walk past a shady looking bar it
catches Sam's eye. The people entering and leaving
look as if they were there for more than just
drinks, and the smell of tobacco smoke gives the
impression the proprietors of this establishment
are more than willing to let a few minor laws be
broken.

"Hey wait a moment Rox. I'd like to check in
here for a bit."

"Is this the kind of establishment a young
Venusian should be influenced by."

"You've been around worse, besides this is for me, and these are my kind of people."

Roczi reluctantly agrees, and it doesn't take long for Sam to find his way into a back room poker game. Unfortunately, Roczi is left in the front to fend for herself as men try to pick up on her not realizing she is a machine. If they did know, it probably wouldn't matter anyway. Eventually Roczi loses her patients and enters the back room.

"Let's go Sam. I didn't drag you down here to abandon me in a bar."

"But I'm up Rox, I gotta give these guys a chance to win back their money. It wouldn't be ethical if I didn't."

"Of course your up. Your way out of their league Sam."

Roczi's words ring true to the three men he's playing. They quickly stand up, and leave the room grumbling to themselves.

"Why did you do that?" Sam asks Roczi.

"Cause you left me at the bar by myself, looking like a prostitute."

"Did you get any good offers?" Sam asks with a smile on his face.

"Let's go, and yes I did," Roczi replies as she leaves the room.

"Don't forget my cut."

"You're a jerk Sam."

They plan to end the day at the ball park. Sam is a huge baseball fan, and Roczi knew he would like to take in a game. It is a Mars League game and Sam is happy to see it's being played by humans. A.I. games just aren't as interesting to Sam, because he knows machine players have to enable performance crippling programs to avoid day long first innings. To Sam it's like a bunch of players on the field trying to throw a game.

It's a close game. The Martian league is full of great players that just couldn't break through and stay at the top level of play on Earth, so they come to Mars to play everyday. After the sixth inning Sam starts feeling hungry, and the venders hotdogs just don't sound good to him. Sam has gotten spoiled and he wants to find something at the concession stands on the concourse.

"I'll be back Rox. Just going to get something to eat."

"What's wrong with what the venders are selling? I thought hotdogs are what people ate at these events."

"I just don't feel like a hotdog."

"Fine, but I'm coming with you."

"I understand. It's difficult for a girl to part with my company."

"Especially when that girl is worried you will find a back-room poker game and abandon her... Again."

The two walk up the steps to the concessions and look for the shortest line when Roczi notices a group of women looking at them.

"Hey Sam, would you know why there is a group of women looking at us?"

Sam takes a look and see's Jessica with some of her friends. She turns her head and acts as if she doesn't notice them as they walk away.

"That's Jessica. The woman I was out with last night," Sam informs Roczi.

"She's pretty, and I'm sure she has the wrong idea about us. You should talk to her."

"Nah. It would give the wrong impression. Like I'm doing something wrong."

"And not doing anything makes a different impression?"

Sam pauses and looks at Roczi.

"I don't feel like putting the effort in to explain."

"Oh, I hope that works out for you," She say's cynically.

Sam orders a bottled water and some Mongolian beef from the concession stand. Then they find a table on the concourse. The seventh inning starts and Sam appears fixated on the game. It's a real pitchers dual, with lots of strike outs and only three scores throughout the whole game, all on single home runs.

Sam's attention is only interrupted when Roczi receives a message on her communicator.

"We need to get back to the escape," Roczi tells Sam.

"Why?" Sam asks.

"There is a cloaked vessel hailing the Escape. They want to make contact with you."

"How could anyone find the escape?" Sam asks clearly surprised.

"I don't know, and Rizac says they are from the Bigan-Nictwar system."

There is a slight pause as Sam tries to piece together an explanation, but he can think of none.

"Time to get back Rox. I've had enough normal life for one day."

They leave the ballgame Sam was so interested in, and immediately head back to the escape. Although they enjoyed the day out, Sam is once again happy to get back to the unknown.

Reacquainted

Roczi and Sam leave Mars heading back to Sam's hidden space station, or what was once thought to have been a hidden space station. The November's sensors are wide open looking for signs of anything, but nothing is found.

The Escape is still cloaked, as is the November, but for Sam to dock with the station they will both have to disengage their cloaks. This will leave them vulnerable to any ships that may be nearby.

"What do you think Rox? Should we disengage our cloak and hope the hidden ship has no ill will toward us."

"They could be waiting to attack. I think we should wait and take some more precautions," Roczi advises Sam.

"I was actually hoping you would say yes, but since you have concerns we will wait."

"No. Don't mind me. You're the captain," Roczi tells Sam.

"Oh good. I'm dying to see who's trying to contact me."

"I only hope the dying doesn't turn out to be literal. Contacting the Escape now."

Roczi contacts Rizac on the escape and both disengage their cloaks. The docking goes off with nothing interesting or strange happening. Once onboard Sam and Roczi quickly make their way to the stations bridge to see what Rizac has found.

"What do you have for me Rizac?" Sam asks.

"Just this hail from a cloaked vessel. We've received it about every 15 minutes for the last 3 hours and we are due to get another one any minute now."

"Do we have any reason to believe it is hostile?"

"No, but I have determined the vessel is either Theon or Mirancris, and I have no idea how they found our location."

"Send out our own hail and let's see what happens," Sam tells him.

"Right away. I'm curious to find out myself," Rizac replies.

Roczi looks at the two organics and determines that Sam's contact plan is a little to haphazard for her, so she attempts to put some kind of backup plan in place.

"Very good you two. I'm going to prep the November for emergency evacuation. You know, our hidden base of operations has been located, and we were recently involved in stopping a Theon or Mirancris invasion of a Human military base.... And Rizac, what kind of ship did you say hailed us?" Roczi asks in a condescending way.

"The ship is either a Theon or Mirancris vessel," He answers.

"Good idea Rox. Glad your on top of it," Sam says as if he doesn't notice her tone.

Roczi then leaves the bridge and heads back to the November shaking her head with a clear look of disdain on her face.

"The hail has been sent Sam," Rizac informs him.

A few moments pass before the hail is answered.

"Sam Stix, please present an internal docking bay. We would like to come aboard and discuss a business transaction."

Sam then takes the communicator and makes a request of his own.

"Vessel you need to identify yourself."

"This is the Tyzon. Please prepare an internal docking bay."

Rizac and Sam look at each other and nod their heads as Roczi walks back into the room.

"Bring them in Rizac," Sam tells him.

"Tyzon, follow the beacon inside the docking bay."

A look of amazement comes over Roczi's face.

"I can't believe this! Now I'll get us some weapons. You do realize the combat droids are gone, don't you Sam?" Roczi asks. Then she walks back out to the armory.

The vessel uncloaks and reveals itself to be a Mirancris luxury spacecraft, and not a military or government ship. Rizac is quick to recognize the high priced space craft.

"That is a very fine shuttle Sam. Not a war machine at all. Whom ever is inside that shuttle is very wealthy, and more than likely very powerful."

"Then lets get them onboard and see what they
are offering. Stay here at the helm. Rox and I will
greet them at the bay."

Sam meets Roczi in the corridor just before
the docking bay were she hands him a .50 caliber
semi automatic pistol and two extra magazines.

"A fire arm," Sam says curiously.

"Yes. I normally prefer the magnetic weapons,
but I like what you did on 4 Vesta with a firearm.
You looked cool, and I think it intimidated our
enemies there."

"Thank you. I'm glad you thought so."

"It will also take attention away from me and
improve my odds," Roczi tells Sam as she smiles.

Sam puts his gun away as they approach the bay
door.

"What are you carrying Rox?"

"A nice, quite, fully automatic, magnetic
trident submachine gun," She says with an even
larger smile on her face this time.

As the door unlocks and opens, Sam has to get in
his last word.

"I'd still give me the upper hand," He tells her.

Roczi just lets out a small laugh and watches the ship as it appears beyond the bay doors. The ship is sleek, crimson, and beautiful. It barely manages to fit in the docking bay, and is shaped something like the number three laying on its side. It's bridge would be the center point, and luckily the ship wasn't hostile, cause the outer points of the ship appear to have been modified into internal weapon bays.

Sam gets Rizac on the communicator.

"Rizac, Can you tell me more about this ship."

"It's a high end Mirancris ship. Something like your exotic Italian vessels."

"So someone important should be coming out?"

"I would suspect as much, but it is possible it's just an heir or heiress. We have those in the Bigan-Nictwar system as well."

"Either way they will have money, so I'm interested."

An exterior door opens on the ship and three metallic blocks come out. Connected only by a force field, the blocks unfold to form a silver three step stairway to the bay floor. Sam and Roczi have never seen anything like this. They are Impressed, but at the same time they believe it's a bit much.

"A simple ramp, or stairway would have done," Sam says to Roczi.

"Yes, but that is really cool."

"Yeah, I want that feature," Sam says to Roczi.

A well dressed Mirancris male begins making his way down the stairs. Right away the glossy black skin and slithering red stripe give away his identity. Suphran has tracked down Sam and his crew for unknown reasons, and now he walks down the stairs and approaches Sam and Roczi. Puzzled and amazed by his arrival, Sam and Roczi take a short glance at each other to confirm what they both see, then turn their attention back to their guest.

"Suphran! I'm surprised to see you. How and why have you found me?" Sam asks.

"I have questions, statements, and requests myself. We should talk in a more comfortable setting. This may take a while," Suphran tells Sam.

"We'll talk in the briefing area. Please come with me."

Sam gives a gesture to Roczi, but she already knows to stay with the ship.

Sam and Suphran enter the briefing room and take their seats at the table across from each other. The room had been adorned by Rizac, and certain familiarities don't go unnoticed by the brilliant strategist.

It's a rustic looking area with hard wood floors, wooden beams, walls, and an oak table with a halo-projector in the center. The walls of the briefing room have artworks on them as well, Including art from the Bigan-Nictwar system. Suphran is quick to notice.

"You have art from my system on your walls. How did you obtain them," Suphran asks.

"Prints I received during some of my latest deployments. I only recently gained ownership of this station and thought it a possibility to host Mirancris and or Theon. I was apparently right."

"Sam I would like to get right to it. Well before I made contact with your kind I had all Human intel agencies and possible envoy's or spies put in our data bases. You never turned up, but you where involved in Humanities biggest development since the advent of artificial intelligence. Maybe even a bigger advent. I needed to know why."

"What have you found?"

"I have found nothing, but facts are really only needed for proof. I merely need to see the obvious. You are a contractor, and your assistant isn't what she seems either."

"That is very observant of you. I truly am impressed, but I already know about Roczi," Sam tells Suphran.

Sam can see the shape of Suphran's eyes change, but it is hard for him to read this very intelligent alien. Was this slight pursing of the eyes caused by curiosity, disappointment that he couldn't use this knowledge to his advantage, or was it simply amusement? Sam would like to believe it is amusement.

"You too wondered why such an advanced A.I. learning about Humanity would take a position with so little Human interaction. I don't blame you Sam. She is more qualified than you in every way, except that you are Human."

"I thought it possible she may be a Venusian agent, but I just seen it as way to get a highly qualified assistant for next to nothing. She may be investigating me, but she has saved my life many times, and not made a single mistake. If she did manage to get any information out of me it was well worth it. Besides, I don't think any info I have is that valuable. Everything is eventually found out anyway."

"That may be one way of looking at it, and it is somewhat similar to how Commander Kaens looks at

things. I tend to think it maybe a little short
sighted. Just a conclusion based on experience."

"You still haven't told me why you are here
Suphran."

Suphran stands up and places a small disc on
the table. Out of the disc deploys a short
hologram. Sam recognizes the figure as Commander
Kaens of the Mirancris military. Then Suphran
begins telling his story.

"You may recognize Commander Kaens. A highly
decorated military strategist, brilliant, extremely
eccentric, and a traitor to his people."

"Yes I recognize him. Isn't he an opponent of
yours?"

"We had different ideas of how we should have
fought the war, but now he is an adversary of all
Mirancris. He may be an adversary of every
intelligent species we know of."

"Really. Tell me more."

"I believe he was the architect behind the
attack on 4 Vesta. I began to investigate strange
activity that cannot be discussed, but needless to
say it all leads to him. Kaens escaped custody with
the help of some of his coconspirators, and I want
him found."

"Why come to me? You have the military to look
for him."

"We have nothing that could lead to his
location, and I believe he may be in command of two
ships. A warship and the Infinite."

"Does the Warship happen to be the Gate's
End?"

"Yes. It was from the Gate's End that I
followed you to this station. I believe Kaens had
the Infinite taken, and some how took the Gate's
End as well. I assume he had agents planted on the
Infinite, but I have no idea how he could have
taken the warship," Suphran manages to mix small
truths with large lies.

Although Suphran is convincing, Sam has his
doubts, and the question of why Suphran had sought
Sam out still had not been answered.

"I still don't know how you expect me to find
Kaens. You know more about him than I do."

"You have the means to locate him. I do not."

"What means is that?" Sam asks.

"Roczi."

"My A.I. assistant that you don't trust is the means to find him? Once again, please enlighten me," Sam requests.

"I believe Kaens will look to recruit mercenaries, and I believe he will utilize the best, most efficient mercenaries he can acquire."

"He will want machines. It makes sense."

"It's the only possible lead I can think of. As you said, I know Kaens and he will try to acquire A.I. mercenaries. I'm willing to advance you half of your payment and give you whatever equipment you need to help me locate him."

"What kind of money and equipment are we talking?"

"Eight million. You get the equipment and first half now."

"What kind of equipment?" Sam asks.

"A trans warp communications device. It's much more efficient than the silly probes you've been using, but it's also far more limited. It only sends a signal to members through an isolated network. I also have a formula to enhance Human performance. I assume you can replicate it here."

"Sounds interesting. What about cloaking equipment, and what do you want done after we locate him?"

"I can give you personal cloaking equipment now. As for your ship, we just don't have the time. I want the Infinite. He has top level scientists and may have Human hostages onboard. I need to know where they are when you find them. I'm not terribly worried about the Gate's End."

"I'll find him and the ship, but I feel like I should let you know, I don't fully believe you," Sam tells Suphran.

"I'm not paying you to believe me. I'm paying you to find Kaens and the Infinite. One more thing I should warn you of. What you may find on infinite could be disturbing to say the least. Some of our leading bioengineers were on the ship and Kaens has been known to take things to far."

Sam takes a brief pause to think about what Suphran has just said. A few horrible thoughts fly through his mind, but Sam never loses composure.

"I understand, and I have an added request of my own," Sam tells Suphran.

"What is your request."

"The stairway into your ship. I want to be the first Human with that feature on his vessel."

"Once this job is complete, you will be."

The Window

Suphran and his beautiful Mirancris ship leave the Escape, but a strange excitement still exists on the station. Sam is already developing a way to find and get onboard one of Kaens' vessels, but all of them involve a huge commitment from his friend and assistant Roczi. It's more commitment than a contractor could ask of an employee, and to much to ask of a friend. Sam now has a reason and a need to ask Roczi to become a full partner. Sam has been wanting to offer Roczi a partner position to ensure she stays on with him, but now the necessity and opportunity have arrived.

Sam walks from the docking bay back to the Escape's briefing room. Upon arrival at the briefing room he requests Roczi's presence via his communicator. Roczi quickly agrees and begins to make her way there. In the meantime Sam grabs a seat and tries to find a comfortable position. He crosses his legs and leans from one side to the other. Sam comes to understand that he is just to excited to sit when Roczi enters the briefing room.

"So what can I help you with Sam?"

"Before our most recent assignments you were integral, but your role has been changing. Growing actually. I could not have saved 4 Vesta without you, and now I have accepted another contract. One that I cannot do without you. In fact, I can't even start without you."

"I do appreciate your acknowledgement Sam, but I'm more interested in this next assignment."

"Just a moment Rox. That's what I'm getting at. I've been wanting to offer this to you for a while, but now I can't ask you to proceed further without having you as a full partner."

"You're offering me a full partnership, into your... unorthodox field of contracting?"

"Yes I am."

"I appreciate it Sam, but I have not completed my Observance, and you have a tendency to get yourself into some highly illegal situations that I don't want to be prosecuted for," Roczi tells Sam in a humorous way.

"I know you're not just fulfilling your Observance Rox. I've known this for some time. Hell, even Suphran knew."

Roczi smiles a bit wider then pulls out a chair and has a seat.

"How long have you known Sam."

Sam then leans back in his chair.

"I hired you expecting as much. I figured hiring a highly programmed Venusian intelligence operative as an assistant would pay off. I was right."

"I thought there may be a low probability of this, but it has paid off for both of us."

"It has, but I need you one-hundred percent on board with me now. I need you, and you know with Van Tellure, Fomn, and now Suphran onboard with us we could be pivotal in the future of all life in the galaxy."

"Sounds to me like you only need a contact representing the most feared force in the known galaxy. I can be of great service to us there."

"Yes. I just need to hear you say you're with me on this Rox."

There is a short pause as Roczi then leans back in her chair, and smiles again.

"I already am Sam. I talked to Dequ-9, the head of the Venusian Special Objectives Division, or VSOD, after 4 Vesta. I let her know that my employment with them is over. My reason for leaving, I thought I could be more useful to the whole of the galaxy with you."

Sam looks at Roczi with amazement on his face.

"You told her that Rox? Do you really believe that?"

"I did, and I do... And before you ask, yes, I'm serious," She tells Sam.

Sam stands up and walks up next to Roczi.

"So you will accept a partnership?"

Roczi stands as well and makes a few statements of her own.

"I don't know Sam. Like I said, you get yourself in a lot of illegal situations and I disagreed with your decision to let the unknown vessel onboard the Escape."

"Then It sounds like I need to bring a little of your wisdom into my rash decision making. Rox, your my best friend and I trust no one more."

"You trust me after I kept the VSOD thing from you? It sounds like the bar is set a little low, but I will be a part of it with you."

The two share a smile and a laugh as Roczi accepts the partnership, and Roczi's role has just grown immensely.

The plan Sam and Roczi decide on will have them back on Venus with Roczi posing as an A.I. mercenary. There they will wait for one of Kaens men to recruit her like Suphran is expecting. Sam and Roczi are hoping for some assistance from her former administrator at the VSOD, Dequ-9. The assistance isn't because they need it. Both Sam and Roczi can locate a general call for contract mercenaries, but this is how Roczi will try and coordinate a rapport between their team and the VSOD.

Leaving the Escape, Sam and Roczi bring Rizac with them. They know that once they get on one of Kaens ships his expertise could be very valuable. Getting to Venus is much simpler than getting to Earth. For one thing, there is no customs station. Navigating through Venus' eight-hundred degree atmosphere is believed to kill any possible alien microbes. On top of that, the machines just haven't found a rational reason to fear organic life.

Hours later, the November enters the Venusian atmosphere slowly to avoid unnecessarily added heat as she flies through her thick dense clouds. The November nears it's rocky surface and the extent of Venus' volcanos become visible. Hell is what Sam thinks of as they move through the Venusian sky. For nearly an hour they move through her lower atmosphere till they reach an entrance to one of the A.I.'s subterranean cities.

They descend into the city through a large corridor. The first large iris door leads to one short downward sloping passage, followed by another. The passages are very dimly lit till the final iris opens, and an awe inspiring city is revealed.

The city's silver sky scrappers are actually beautiful inhabited pillars nearly two kilometers high, with smaller buildings seemingly floating In the air between them. The beautiful ceiling-sky changes slowly between night and day, and the pillared housing with its floating shops and commercial buildings are amazing. The city floor is saved for art galleries, trees, flowers, and even different types animals from earth. The things Humans seem to take for granted the A.I.'s hold most high. Even being on the solid surface is considered a place of prestige amongst them, as opposed to the common Human conception of penthouses and beach front property. Solid sturdy ground is prized by the machines.

The city is called Persia, in honor of one of earths first civilizations, and it also happens to be Roczi's home. She still has her apartment in this city, and it will be their base of operations till they depart.

The November lands in a huge, hanging ceiling-sky docking bay with thousands of other ships. Then the three leave the November en route to Roczi's apartment. Once they arrive, they set up and begin working quickly. Sam opens contact links searching for active calls for mercenary contracts, and for the whereabouts of known A.I. mercenaries.

"Links are setup Rox. I think it's time you made contact with your old administrator," Sam says to Roczi.

"If you want me to make the call you're gunna have to stay out of site."

Sam and Rizac understand and leave the room so Roczi can contact Dequ-9. Uncertain how the conversation will go, they hope for the best as she reaches Dequ-9 on the communicator.

"Roczi, I am surprised to here from you. What can I do for you?" Dequ-9 asks.

She is yet another beautiful A.I. in the form of a female, with long black hair and green eyes. She even wares the completely unnecessary accessory of cat-eye glasses. This shows the extent of Human culture on the Venusian A.I.s.

"I'm looking into a possible alien build up of Venusian mercenaries. Can you give me leads into high yield mercenary contact channels?" Roczi asks.

"I could, but I am struggling to understand why I should. It could even be a strategic error to aid you with your request."

"I assure you, it will be in all of our best interests to help Sam and I in this endeavor. I will pass any pertinent information on to the VSOD if we receive assistance. This will be free of the usual Human charges as well. You will also be receiving this information without having to remove operatives from their assignments. It would be a positive action for both parties."

"I agree. I will send you the information. On top of that, the VSOD will pay seventy-five-thousand for the information up front. You and your counterpart may be able to use it for your operation, or future ones. Is there anything else we can assist you with?"

"Yes. We could also use two organic transport boxes."

"They will be at your location within ten minutes."

"Thank you Dequ-9."

"You are welcome Roczi."

The conversation ends and the information, equipment and funds have essentially been acquired.

Sam walks back into the room with an amazed look on his face.

"That was it?" Sam asks, as he and Rizac enter the room.

"That was all that was necessary. Quick and efficient. Did you expect something different?" Roczi replies.

"I didn't really expect anything. I was just surprised it was so easy. You made us another seventy-five-thousand credits, and you didn't even have to ask. Do Venusians really part with their cash that quick,"

"We don't have the need for it Humans do. Now all we have to do is wait for the call for mercs, if it comes."

"It will come. This is nice Rox, but maybe we could go somewhere? Let Rizac see a little bit of Venus. Your choice."

"I like the idea. How about we show Rizac a little culture? Lets go to the Arts Cathedral."

Sam sighs, but understands he gave Roczi the choice.

"Ok fine, but next time I choose."

"That's next time. This one is mine. Just give me a few minutes with my cats."

Roczi proceeds to baby talk her cats for nearly five minutes before Sam and Rizac persuade her to leave. Then they are out to see what Venus has to offer.

There are many different types of A.I.'s as well as humans within Persia's city limits. In the short time the war has been over the three species new to the system have already began diplomatic relations with Venusian leaders. Rizac is quickly recognized as Theon by the Venusian populous, but the machines mind their manners and leave the newcomer alone.

They soon arrive on the floor of the city and the arts cathedral. Gothic in design and huge, the building leaves Rizac intrigued. Sam is as well, but he chooses not to let Roczi know of his interest.

Once inside the museum they see the beautiful white interior is even more impressive than the exterior. Paintings, sculptures, photographs, and other works are on the walls, or suspended in the air. The art works from Earth are clearly most prized here. To Sam's eye the machines have produced superior art, but only when the artist are not imitating Human works. They look at the first level of mostly Human works for over an hour till

Sam finally gets tired of looking at the art he's known for most of his life.

"Rox, it's time to let Rizac see some Venusian works. Let's take him to one of the other levels."

"But there is still so much more of Humanity's art to be seen," Roczi says to Sam.

"Yes, but I think Venusians under appreciate their own. We should get an outsiders opinion. What do you say Riz?"

Rizac looks at them both and then looks up through the transparent ceiling at all the Venusian art they still haven't seen.

"We could be going through these levels and corridors for days before I see everything, and I would like to see some Venusian art before we head out on our next mission."

"Alright Rizac. Let's see what you think of Venusian art," Roczi says to him.

A transparent platform comes down near a pillar. They step onboard it, and the platform takes them up several levels to see what the machines have contributed to the world of art. The different paintings and sculptures are almost entirely Venusian on the upper levels, and the pieces differ greatly in style and variety. Rizac is completely intrigued by the works. He enjoys comparing the differences and similarities between, not just the art here in the museum, but the works he remembers from the Mirancris luxury ship Divine Gate before the war turned her into the warship Gate's End. Turns out, Rizac is a true art aficionado.

Roczi's communicator goes off, and she is happy to find It's the call for mercenaries they where expecting and counting on. They will have to continue their museum tour another time, since their objective is about to get a step closer.

"So what do you think Rizac? Do you have a preference, Human or Venusian?" Roczi asks.

"I really don't think I have seen enough to decide. We'll have to comeback another time. Hopefully soon," He tells her.

"Let's go. I have to show you how to pack up, and prepare to go," Roczi says.

"Pack up? What do you mean?" Sam asks.

"I'll have to show you back to the apartment. It's how I'm getting you onboard. You'll see."

When they arrive back at Roczi's apartment there are several large boxes that weren't there when they left. Two of which are metallic, and larger than the others.

"What are these?" Sam asks.

"Supplies, and your tickets in," Roczi answers.

"How is that?"

"The two large metallic boxes are called organic crates. They were developed to smuggle Humans through customs sensors, just in case we ever needed to use them. They prohibit the typical life sign flags from being found by sensors. It's more full proof than hoping they won't scan for life signs."

"They look like coffins," Sam tells Roczi.

The look on Rizac's face makes it clear, the idea of squeezing into one of those boxes designed for a Human's much smaller frame does not make him happy.

"If you would please, could you two inventory the equipment in the crates? I have to locate the meeting point and make sure I'm not recognized," Roczi tells Sam and Rizac.

The equipment crates are full of high grade technology like cloaking devices and sensors. They are nice but Sam always has a preference for opening weapons crates. Dequ-9 even sent provisions for Humans, including enhancement suits and field armor. The equipment is inventoried and recorded, and the help from the VSOD increases Sam's confidence in the mission.

A short time passes, then Roczi comes out of the next room looking entirely different. A few inches taller, with a completely different facial structure, and short blonde hair, Roczi manages to surprise both Sam and Rizac. She looks the part of a mercenary in black tactical gear, Including a tight black t-shirt, black cargo pants and tactical holsters.

"I have a location. It's a large theatre on the other side of the planet. It's in a city called Antech," Roczi informs the others.

Antech was the first settlement on Venus, and it is currently the most populous. It has many different venues that may be rented out. Most often these venues are used by Humans for different corporate events, but this one will clearly be different.

They fly the November well above the Venusian atmosphere to avoid as much of the hot thick air as possible. The planet is also much more pleasant to look at from outside of its air space, and In just under an hour the November plunges back into the hell that is the Venusian atmosphere. Roczi locates the city's entrance much quicker this time, and within minutes they enter the city's surface corridor.

275

Entering the city, it is clear that this is one of Venus' older cities. The city is a little darker and the ceiling sky is not a replicated view of the stars threw clouds. Simple reflective tiles and bright lights make up the ceilings here. It is still pretty, but not nearly as impressive as the city of Persia. Antech is also substantially larger than Persia as well, in fact Antech is nearly five times as large and houses over five million in her pillars. That number includes over two-hundred-thousand Humans.

The theatre is quickly found by Roczi, and the November docks in the ceiling sky. Roczi knows she will have to leave Sam waiting, and although it will bother Sam, it is necessary for Roczi to attend the theatre alone.

"Rox, guess you're on your own for this part."

"I have this down Sam. Don't worry, I'll get you up to speed when I get back."

"I know you got this. See you soon, but I'm letting you know the anticipation is killing me," Sam tells Roczi.

Roczi leaves the the November on foot en route to the theatre. Before she even steps off the ramp she notices A.I. mercenaries in the area. For the most part, they seem to be heading to the theatre, but some are staying back keeping eyes on their ships. Roczi enters a lift with about two dozen other A.I.s. Most A.I.'s choose to look Human, but not these ones. Like the mercenary on the Gargoyle, these A.I.'s want their enemies to know they are machines. Exposed steel construction and armor plating is how these A.I.'s present themselves.

Roczi takes a lift down to a walkway around the theatre, which sits suspended over a kilometer above the city floor. As the lift descends, Roczi can see others approaching the theatre from other lifts and walkways. By the time she arrives the walkways are congested with machine warriors looking to see what the contract offers. Then the doors open to the theatre and the mercenaries calmly enter. Roczi waits and lets some of the larger machines go in first. She counts nearly five-hundred-four mercenaries in the auditorium before she takes her seat near the back the doors close.

Then the lights dim and the theatre gets quiet. On the stage curtains are pulled and a figure appears. It's a Human figure in tactical gear. His face is obscured by the large round brim hat he wears as he hangs his head over a podium. Then he raises his head revealing his identity to the crowd. Roczi is stunned to see that Nico is alive, and recruiting mercenaries for Kaens.

Peeking In

Shocked to see Nico amongst the living and confused by his recruiting for Kaens, Roczi wants to inform Sam right away, but she refrains. She knows one of the mercenaries may pick up the transmission and blow her cover before they can even get started. Just as shocking as his reemergence is his appearance. Roczi is stunned to see Nico's eyes. Oversized and black, his eyes change color and patterns while he speaks. Then Roczi recognizes the Laurine language coming through his eyes. She momentarily questions her earlier facial scan, but it is definitely Nico.

Nico brings his attention to the audience and addresses the mercenaries. He is very strait forward and direct as he speaks, and he should be. It's not easy to fool a machine, and when they find out it Is trouble for the deceiver.

"Let me get right to the point. The make up of the known galaxy has changed dramatically, and with it, so have it's opportunities. Trade routes are about to boom. Power players, such as my employer, are making their moves, but my employer is willing to pay, and with more than just money. I know your next question, and yes my employer has more than enough money to fill all of your accounts with credits."

The crowed sighs in relief and laughs at Nico's humorous remark, but he has only just begun. As it turns out he also knows how to sell a crowd. Nico let's the offer and opportunity speak for itself.

"We are in control of two capitol ships. One of witch is a proven battle ready vessel from the Bigan-Nictwar war, and the second is a special capitol ship that only a select few will see. The secondary incentive, in our minds, is the 300,000,000 credits that will be split between all involved. That could be over 600,000 credits to each of you. That is if all of you stay. Course those with there own vessels receive a ten-percent bonus taken from the general fund, and any advanced weapons or technology can be purchased at our prices. But this may not be your primary motivation to join us. Along the way we will find different moons and planets only suitable for A.I. settlement and no other. For a price we will help you homestead these areas. These could be very lucrative in the extensive life of an A.I., especially with the population limitations on Venus. Those of you who are interested in our offer and who have their own vessels can find our ship on the dark side of mercury for the next twenty-four hours, and those without can find shuttles in Antech bay 12-G-104 for the next twenty hours. If

279

there are any questions please direct them to the com. Thank you and I hope to see you onboard," Nico finishes his pitch and simply walks off stage.

It's a great offer for the mercenaries, and Roczi knows the vast majority of those who attended will accept. She hurries out of the theatre to inform Sam about their new destination, and of course the reemergence and new role Nico new plays.

The lifts and walkways leaving the theatre are crowded with machines, but there is no excitement from the machines as they leave the theatre. Any Human given the opportunity to receive over half-a-million credits and explore the galaxy with the option of claiming their own part of distant space would be very excited, but these are machines who know the advantages of being just that. Even the vast majority of A.I.'s would come out at least exhibiting interest, but these A.I.'s are interested more so in the fact that they are machines, and therefore superior. They all heard the same offer and retained it, so there is no need to talk about it.

The November is still docked in the upper bays of Antech with Sam and Rizac onboard, and as A.I. mercenaries walk past the ship, Roczi approaches. The November's ramp lowers, but Sam Rizac and are not waiting at the top to greet her. Instead they are waiting on the bridge observing the A.I. mercenaries around them.

"Thank you for the greeting guys," Roczi tells them as she enters the bridge.

"Sorry Rox. I was trying to get I.D.'s on as many mercs as possible."

"Don't worry about that Sam. I have I.D.'s and dossiers on nearly all that attended. The only exceptions are a few newcomers."

"I am glad to here that, but I have to say the mercenaries I've I.D.ed so far are very formidable. I'd hate to be on the opposing fighting force," Sam tells Roczi.

"Well then I'd suggest switching teams and joining Kaens, cause as far as recruitment goes it doesn't get any better,"

"How many mercs and what is Kaens offering," Rizac inquires.

"I counted five-hundred-four mercenaries, and from what we were offered, I am confident any who were serious will accept a contract. I'm guessing approximately four-hundred-ninety plus mercs will be on Kaens' pay roll with-in 20 hours."

"A force like that would be very formidable," Sam adds.

"That's why no one can know what we are doing here. If any of these mercenaries realize we're here spying on Kaens we will probably be tortured, disassembled, and destroyed," Roczi tells Sam and Rizac.

"Well, we can't let that happen. I still haven't received my luxurious Mirancris stairway for the November," Sam reminds Roczi.

"I sincerely hope you're joking Sam."

"I'm actually only half joking. It would be nice to have one."

"Let's go. We need to get to the dark side of Mercury. We have less than 20 hours," Roczi tells them.

"That sounds like plenty of time."

Roczi gives Sam a disapproving look then quickly and roughly lifts off, making Sam stumble.

With all the preparations already made, they depart the city of Antech en route to the dark side of Mercury.

Mercury has very little significance to either A.I.'s or Humans. The surface has several small instillations near the poles, but even those are almost exclusively for mining and science operations. The rest of the planet's surface has temperatures to extreme for Human settlement, and the machines are just more focused on subterranean

Venus. It's low population and large number of mining and warehouse districts make it a popular destination for illegal transactions. Although very little happens there, something very large is about to happen just a few kilometers off Mercury's surface. Hiding in the shadow of the planet is a huge armor plated warship. The ship is awaiting the arrival of the best combat assassins this system can offer. A group of killers without a heartbeat, without hesitation, and with very few limitations.

The November approaches the planet's night side with dozens of others, but no ship is detected. Roczi runs a series of scans throughout the area, but only finds a handful of small anomalies. They know a ship is there, the scans are merely to see check the origin of the ship. The low levels of anomalies can only be from a Mirancris or Theon vessel since Human cloaks are not yet as advanced.

"What kind of scans are Theon and Mirancris ships capable of Rizac? Can they scan for life signs from this distance?" Sam asks.

"Yes, but it would have given away the ships position."

"We only have one shot at this, so lets get in the crates. Rox, the helm is all yours," Sam tells his crew.

Sam and Rizac walk back to their quarters and
into the organic crates. They have no choice but to
be patient as Roczi waits for the ship to appear.
Well over an hour passes before the ship comes out
of cloak. The first thing to appear are the giant
metal plates suspended around the warship. Then the
actual ship becomes visible, and Roczi recognizes
it right away. The Gate's End has made it's way to
Earth's solar system, and it is obtaining the means
to make war. Once again, Roczi wants to tell Sam
what she sees but the crates meant to prevent
scanning systems from peaking in also prevent
communication signals from penetrating. Then
instructions begin transmitting from the Gate's
End.

Roczi is directed to bring the November to an
internal docking bay, as are all the other
approaching ships. This time the Gate's End appears
brighter than the last time they seen it. It may be
that the war has ended, or possibly the change in
administration, But it's more likely that Kaens'
wants the mercenaries to see some of it's
brilliance. The change makes the Gate's End a
little more welcoming than it was the first time
Roczi encountered it. Whatever the reason for it's
new look, it does not matter. Roczi is taking the
November back onboard.

Roczi settles the ship into the docking bay
and the doors close, but the bay does not fill with
air. Machines don't need it. After they land Sam
and Rizac exit their cases and meet with Roczi on

the bridge to go over the plan. They use the
November's sensors to scan the Gate's End and Rizac
uses his extensive knowledge of the ship to help
map out the ships important control and service
areas, focusing on their location and proximity to
the bridge and other bays.

"All Suphran wants is to find Kaens and the
Infinite. We're gunna have to wait and see what the
next move is gunna be?" Roczi tells Sam and Rizac.

"Commander Kaens will be on the Infinite. I
doubt he would be here. Not with all the activity
in this system," Sam tells Roczi.

"How sure are you this ship will take us
there?" Rizac asks.

"I'm almost certain. Kaens will want to see
his progress. He'll want to see what he's
purchased."

"Then we won't make a move till we find the
Infinite, and I don't think we shouldn't inform
Suphran till we have the opportunity to leave
quickly," Roczi says.

"I agree. It's possible Suphran was behind the
attack on 4 Vesta, and If that's the case, he may
just want to destroy the evidence. I don't want to
be in possession of the evidence when it happens,"
Sam adds.

"We also need to find out what happened to the Human diplomats. I have no intention of sentencing them to death for another four million," Roczi tells Sam and Rizac.

She then leaves the November and walks up to the bay's exit. Entering the Corridors of the Gate's End she takes one more look at the November as the door closes.

Sam takes a looks at Rizac and raises an eyebrow.

"Four million. I can't lie Riz. I'm on the fence about it," Sam says as he shrugs his shoulders.

"You truly are a mercenary, and you know what I think of mercenaries Sam."

The Stage

Once Roczi enters the corridor she finds a Laurine mercenary there to escort her. Using the map they scanned from the November and the information Rizac gave her, she determines she is being escorted to a conference hall. As they pass through the corridors nearing the conference hall the number of mercenaries grow till they arrive at their destination.

The conference area is very large, with more than enough seating for the five-hundred expected to attend. As the mercenaries enter Roczi looks around the large room. She is somewhat surprised that the room doesn't have a holographic deck in the center. Instead this conference area is more like an old theatre with all the seats facing a stage at one end. On the stage patiently waiting is Nico. Dressed in black tactical and sitting on a collapsing chair, he enters information into a data device. Occasionally he'll look up and glance at the crowd entering the room with his new alien eyes.

Roczi takes a seat near the center and waits for the presentation to begin. It doesn't take long for all the mercenaries to arrive after that. Nico must have been informed that all who will attend have arrived, cause only sixteen hours into the twenty allotted Nico begins speaking to the crowd.

"Thank you all for arriving so quickly. Your efficiency has put us well ahead of schedule. That is another reason we put so much into having you join us," Nico tells the crowd. Then he continues.

"We will now be leaving this system to rendezvous with our other capitol ship. Most of you will be placed in squads designed for specific purposes. A few of you will be on security details for our leadership. Some will be involved in gunship operations, and I'm sure we have at least a few with the ability to change form. We already have objectives for you."

Roczi hears Niko's last sentence and begins calculating the odds. She wonders if this is an opportunity or a set up.

"Just to be clear, we have plenty of soldiers. Laurine, several different types of genetic and machine assisted constructs will be the bulk of our forces. You will be involved in missions that we cannot afford to fail," Nico tells the A.I. mercenaries.

A screen comes on behind Nico and an image of space appears on it. The image bends on the screen, and Roczi realizes they are already leaving their system. Moments later the image on the screen changes and an orange gas giant with a grey, Ice covered moon are now visible off in the distance.

Roczi then gets an odd message in the form of text code from Rizac. It reads "Roczi, this com is secure. Hidden in the Gate's End's automated systems. If you need to contact Sam or I use this channel."

More at ease having a secure form of communication with the rest of her team, she waits for more information from Nico.

"In your quarters there will be a data device. Use it to submit your dossier. You will now be shown to your quarters, then you can feel free to explore the ship," It is the last statement Nico tells the attendees before they begin leaving the conference hall.

The mercenaries are assigned a quarters by a holographic map that quickly flashes for each individual by the exits. The machines retain the image quickly, but roczi waits. She lets the others out first as she tries to keep a visual on the screen. It is clear the ship is quickly approaching the ice covered moon, as its image gets larger on the screen. The crowd is quickly exiting the room and Roczi positions herself to be one of the last to leave. She tries to watch the screen as they get closer to the moon. Then she see's it, a vessel near the moon. As they get closer she recognizes the dual dome shaped top, and inverted city scape underneath. She gets what she was hoping for just as she leaves the room.

"I have confirmation. We are approaching the Infinite," Roczi sends by text to Sam.

Sam is excited to hear the news, but now he must solve a bigger problem. He has to confirm Kaens presence and discover what happened to the Human envoys, but that can only be accomplished onboard the infinite. Sam also knows he's not going to figure this out with the poor communication he currently has with Roczi. Improving communications will have to take priority.

"Is there any way we can improve com with Roczi?" Sam asks Rizac.

"I can increase bandwidth, but if to much data goes through those channels they may be noticed, intercepted, and traced."

"We're gunna need voice communication. Nothing more, but nothing less either," Sam tells Rizac.

"Got it. I'll increase our stream. I'm just glad you're not partnered up with a Laurine. If I had to send video data through this channel I may not be able to keep it hidden."

"I'm sure we could have it further compressed somehow."

"It would have to be decompressed on her end, and Laurine can't speak audibly," Rizac explains to Sam.

"I think I can find a way to profit off that."

"Not if I beat you to it. It's done. You can speak to her now," Rizac says.

After Rizac increases their data stream and Sam doesn't waist any time getting in contact with Roczi.

"Any ideas how to get on that ship?" Sam asks her.

"I have an idea that may get me there, but it's not full proof."

"Give me the details."

"They are asking for personal dossiers from us to determine assignment. It sounds like a security detail might get me on the ship. They also seem to want A.I.'s with adjusting form ,such as myself for special assignments. I'm guessing those assignments will be kept separate from normal military ops."

"That's how you'll get in. How long will it be before you get your assignment?" Sam asks.

"I haven't arrived at my quarters to submit my dossier yet, but things are moving very rapidly. At this pace we should know within the hour."

"Understood. Keep me informed of your progress. Rizac and I will search for alternatives on our end. You'll be informed on our progress."

With Roczi moving forward with her plan to board the Infinite, Sam and Rizac are left trying to come up with other options. It is immediately realized that getting the November off of the Gate's End unnoticed is where they should begin.

"Rizac, can you disable the sensors to the bay doors?" Sam asks.

"That will be fairly simple. I can do that from inside this docking bay. The real problem will be keeping the power usage in this bay from sending a breach or malfunction signal to the bridge."

"What happens if that occurs?"

"A field goes up till the problem can be diagnosed and fixed, but if that happens we won't get off this ship."

"Can we open the doors without using power or putting up a field?"

Rizac pauses for a moment to think about Sam's question, but he then gives Sam a definitive answer.

"I'm certain I can. We should put on our walking suits. I will have to access the inner hull, and you should be ready for zero atmosphere and gravity as a safety precaution."

"Let's suit up and begin. I'll monitor com chatter, you do your thing. Which consists of everything else," Sam says to Rizac.

"That's fine. Just be ready to get us the hell out of here if we're discovered."

Then the two head back to their quarters and suit up.

Sam just finishes putting on his space suit when he receives an update from Roczi.

"Sam, my dossier has been sent. I'll notify you when I receive my orders."

"Understood Rox. Rizac is working on a way to get the November out undetected. If you can't get onboard we'll fly to the Infinite and find some way in. One way or another, we'll get confirmation."

"I really like your plan-B Sam. Why don't we just proceed with that while I wait safely on the

November. It will be like old times," Roczi kids
Sam.

"Cause It doesn't actually get us onboard."

"Minor details," Roczi replies in a joking
manor.

Minutes later, Rizac and Sam meet at the
entrance ramp of the November, Rizac with a small
box of tools and Sam heavily armed as usual.

"It should only take me about fifteen minutes
to disable the bay sensors, and under an hour on
the doors and field power," Rizac tells Sam.

"How are you going to open the bay doors
without power?"

"They will have power, it will just be
provided by the November, not the Gate's End. I
will need to use a power cell from the November to
operate the doors," Rizac tells Sam.

There is a brief moment of awkward silence as
Sam thinks over this information and how it will
effect his precious ship. Sam looks at the November
and the giant bay doors, then back at Rizac.

"It's a good plan. I'll watch the internal
door while you work," Sam tells him.

Rizac quickly begins working on the door's sensors, removing panels and going strait to what needs to be disabled.

Sam approaches the much smaller internal door, briefly stopping to think about how well things have fallen into place. He was somehow lucky enough to recruit a team member who was literally designed to know everything about the ship he has stowed away on, and now he is waiting for his form changing A.I. crew member to receive orders for an assignment she is seemingly designed for as well. It all seems just a little to perfect, but it gets erie when he receives an update from Roczi.

"Sam, I received my orders. I am to report to a shuttle bay in just under an hour for assignment. It sounds like I'll be en route to the Infinite. I'm headed back to you now for a face to face."

"I'll be waiting for you."

Minutes later Roczi enters the docking bay, but Sam initially doesn't recognize her because she is not in her usual form.

"I'm glad I was able to meet with you before I set out. We don't have much time, and we need to prepare an exit strategy fast," Roczi tells Sam.

"Same here, and I agree. I want you in and out of there as quick as possible. Rizac and I will have the November out of here and ready to get you before long," Sam say as he puts his hand on her shoulder.

"We won't have safe com channels while I'm on the Infinite. Unless things go wrong, you won't hear from me till I'm ready for extraction."

"Rox, If you can't find out what happened to the envoys without exposing yourself, then don't. We're all getting out of this alive, and quite a bit richer."

"I'll get it done Sam. Have the November ready and we will all ride off into the sunset together," Roczi tells Sam in an optimistic tone.

"Good luck Rox," Sam says as he releases her shoulder.

"You too, and keep Riz safe. I like what he has done on the Escape, and I want to see what he can do to my apartment," She says as she turns and walks out of the internal bay door.

"That's not what he does," Sam says as she leaves.

After Roczi walks out, Sam gets that feeling again. That feeling like things are to perfect, and they're being set up. He walks over to Rizac to ask him if he is sure he can get this done, but then changes his mind. No need to put extra pressure on someone else cause he needs reassurance. Sam will keep his concerns to himself so Rizac can stay focused. After all, this wouldn't be the first time Sam followed through with an assignment against his better instincts.

Not to long after, Rizac approaches Sam.

"The bay door sensors are disabled. I'm going into the inner hull to change the door's energy source," Rizac informs Sam.

"Great. Let me know if you need anything. I'll be on the November."

"Making sure she's prepped and ready? Our situation must be more discomforting then I expected."

"No. Prepping is Roczi's thing. I have another thing, but I do want you prepared. Take this," Sam says as he hands Rizac a satchel containing a submachine gun and several grenades.

"Think it may come to that?" Rizac asks.

Sam takes a moment Then looks right at Rizac.

"No."

Rizac is once again confused by Sam, but he realizes it's something he'll have to get used to.

"Alright... I'll notify you when It's
finished. Their shouldn't be complications."

As Rizac walks toward the maintenance panel
leading to the inner hull, Sam walks up the
November's ramp and makes his way to the bridge.
Once there, Sam sits in the captains chair, leans
back, and closes his eyes.

Rizac removes a maintenance panel using a
magnetic tool that releases latches on the other
side of the panel. The slight hiss of a broken seal
can be heard. Then he enters the airlock portion of
the hull access area and manually seals the panel
latches behind him. He feels the large reduction in
artificial gravity as he passes the threshold into
the dark inner hull, but when the final passage is
sealed the the gravity is reduced to zero. Rizac
pulls himself through the inner hull and quickly
finds the bay doors power connection. Just as
quickly as he gets there he disconnects them, but
now comes the hard part. Rizac has to make an alien
ship's bay doors function with a power cell from
the November.

As Rizac works on the doors, Roczi arrives at
her shuttle. Where she finds one other A.I. already
onboard. The machine appears to be a Human male,
but he has an energy signature Instead of life
signs. He is clearly an appearance changing A.I.
like herself. Four more A.I. mercenaries enter the
shuttle minutes after her. They are much larger,
better armored and stronger than the changers.

Roczi determines they must have been chosen for security detail.

What happens next confuses Roczi in a way that a stuns her, something that almost never happens to a machine. Kiten enters the shuttle just after the four larger mercenaries. Roczi has no knowledge of her involvement on 4 Vesta, but finding Suphran's trusted assistant on this rouge vessels is as intriguing as it is disturbing.

Darkness In The Light

With Rizac finishing his sabotage on the giant warship, Roczi in deep cover to conduct further espionage while surrounded by mercenaries, and Sam taking a nap in his familiar and cozy captains chair, the stage has been set. The next set of events will trigger Sam and his team into their next course of action, whatever it may be. If all goes as hoped, Commander Kaens presence will be confirmed and the whereabouts of the Human envoys will be determined. Then Roczi can simply jump ship and Sam can pick her up. Then the crew can make their notifications and return home. If they're discovered, or if Roczi's cover is blown, they may have to kill and fight for their lives to escape the giant capitol ships, and fleeing from five-hundred machine mercenaries and a small army of genetic constructs would not be an easy task.

Sam knows without hidden communications channels on the Infinite Roczi is on her own. Still, Sam is confident Roczi will complete her mission and return safely, but worry has turned his nap into deep thought and planning.

Roczi's shuttle arrives onboard the Infinite a short time after they leave. As she did in the conference room of the Gate's End, she leaves last hoping to catch something from the back of the group as they exit the shuttle. Without speaking, Kiten simply motions for the machines to follow her through the Infinite's huge brightly lit hangar bay toward a grand entryway. Roczi follows the Laurine and five other machines as they approach the interior's main entrance. She hadn't seen this part of the Infinite before and wonders why Suphran chose not to bring Sam and the other envoys through the Infinite's amazing hangar bay. Then it occurs to her, the massive four level hanger houses only thirty shuttles, but nearly eight-hundred fighters and gun ships. Suphran must not have wanted to give the wrong impression.

The polished grand entryway is similar in the style to some of what Rizac has done to the Escape, but in a vastly more grandiose scale. There are a few other noticeable differences as well. Most notable is, parts of it are alive. The pillars breathe, and filter the air like trees, but are as strait and strong as steel beams. In Roczi's A.I. Slanted opinion, this is the most beautiful structure she has ever seen.

They walk on the marbled doors past the living entryway. Then Kiten gets on her communicator and

301

contacts Commander Kaens. The colorful character shapes of the Laurine language flash across Kiten's face, then again across the small screen of her communicator.

"Commander, I have arrived with our specialists," Kiten advises the Commander.

"It's much earlier than I anticipated. Doctor Minger may not be ready," Is Kaens' concerned reply.

"My apologies Commander Kaens. I assumed you wanted things done as quickly as possible."

"Suphran may have tolerated this type of disorganization, but my time frames have a purpose. Now the doctor and I will have to adjust our schedules. Get someone to escort them," The commander states in an angry set of images.

"Then the changers to the labs and the beasts to you Commander?" Kiten says describing the mercenaries.

"Yes."

The conversation ends there, but it leaves a clear impression. Their is already a rift developing in the partnership. Roczi's previous experience with the Laurine has helped her confirm Kaens' presence on the Infinite, and notice the uneasy partnership between Kiten and Kaens. Then two unknown humanoid creatures walk into the corridor. They ate short with matte green and black scaled skin. They also have forward binocular vision with two ghostly white eyes. Kiten directs the creatures to lead Roczi and the other changer to the labs. Then she sends the large steel plated A.I.'s to Kaens.

As they walk through the halls and corridors Roczi further analyzes the new species. They are unarmed, wearing simple black light armor, and haven't yet spoken. Something about them gives Roczi the impression that this species may not be a naturally occurring one, or possibly an altered. It's small stature would minimize supply intake and increase mobility, it's eyes would better determine range, and the reasoning for it's coloring is obvious.

They walk for nearly twenty minutes before one of the creatures takes the four larger machines down another path. Now it's just the one short creature, the other A.I. changer, and Roczi walking down corridors that are quickly loosing their beauty.

As they near the laboratories where they will get their orders, the decorum is getting steadily more simple and basic.

"I go by Desmond. Do you have a name or preferred designation?" The other changer asks, breaking the silence.

Roczi turns her head toward the A.I.. She gives him a glance then looks forward.

"Nessa," Roczi tells him.

"A name! I am relieved. I was concerned I may be working with one of those machine supremacists," Desmond tells her jokingly.

"Guess we both got lucky there. So how did you get into the paid killer game Desmond?"

"My Observance was as concierge at a resort in a still warring area of west Africa. After my service there was complete I decided to try and end the fighting on my own. Less than three years later the fighting had stopped, strangely most of the leadership on both sides had disappeared or became extremely reclusive...," Desmond says as a smile crosses his face, but then he continues.

"How did you spend your Observance?" He asks.

"I worked with a wealthy exporter from Japan. Turned out, he was also smuggling. I chose to continue working for him. It could get exciting at times. What kind of special assignments do you expect they'll have for us us?" Roczi asks right afterward.

"I don't know, but I expect them to want us to blend with the population."

Roczi and Desmond share a short laugh, then are led into a small room with windows on one side. The escort simply motions for them to wait and leaves the two inside.

"We A.I.s make that little creature seem down right mechanical," Desmond tells her.

"True, and it had a mouth. It could have at least tried to be social," Roczi replies with a little laugh afterward.

Desmond's comments amuse Roczi and make her mission a little more enjoyable. He has a personality similar to Sam's, and Roczi is appreciating it.

"I take it you prefer the relaxed approach to taking on stress you don't actually have," Roczi says to him.

"You know being A.I. has immense advantage, but being so close to perfect leaves little to talk about."

"I understand. Sometimes you just have to ...

"Fake it," They both say at the same time.

Then Doctor Minger enters the room from the opposite side. As all Mirancris, he is short with black eyes, but his light grey skin with black and yellow pin-stripes match his double breasted lab coat perfectly.

"I'll need one of you to come with me," Doctor Minger tells them.

"You may get a bit antsy. Go a head," Roczi tells Desmond as she turns to face him.

"I'll see you around," He replies.

Desmond and the Doctor walk back through the door he just entered from. Then Roczi stands and approaches the windows looking into the labs. Inside she sees Doctor Minger take Desmond into another room. Then she begins observing other areas of the labs.

The labs are very clean and organized with Mirancris in lab coats moving around the deeply lowered floor. The lab floor is a story lower the room Roczi is waiting in, but the ceiling is also a story higher. In the center of the massive lab is a three story structure with walkways and scientific devices inside and out. On the bottom floor of the lab a Mirancris in a lab coat walks to the center structure with an automated hard covered cart following. He walks right up next to the structure with the cart, stopping only centimeters away. Then the cart begins quickly transferring metallic rectangular boxes into the structure, but that short distance is all Roczi needs. From a story high peering into a slot about two centimeters wide

she sees the unfortunate confirmation. Labeled as
Human specimens, the crates confirm the fate of the
envoys.

Once again Roczi's previous experience with
the Mirancris has proven immeasurably valuable.
With the final confirmation made, Roczi only needs
to get back to Sam and the November, but Roczi
realizes the best course of action is to stay
inconspicuous till then.

Not to long afterward Desmond and Doctor
Minger emerge from the door. Clearly the heads on
this ship have been briefed on the A.I. Desire to
be direct and strait forward. Roczi timed their
meeting at under four minutes.

"See me when your done," Desmond tells her as
he passes by, then walks out of the room.

"Please come with me Nessa," The doctor tells
her.

"Will I be getting my orders here doctor?"
Roczi asks.

"Yes you will, and we have a bit of intel with
some small equipment to assist you in your
mission."

"Couldn't you just give me the equipment and a
drive with the information?" Roczi asks as they
walk into Doctor Minger's large dark office.

"That was the original plan, but your early arrival had slightly changed them. Lucky for you we have caught up, so here you are," The Doctor tells her as he hands her a small, rectangular, metallic box.

"The drive inside will tell you everything you need to know. Even where your new quarters are. We are done here," He tells Roczi.

"Thankfully that was shorter than I expected."

"If you are judging our meetings time frames by my previous meeting. Desmond was unexpectedly talkative for an A.I." The doctor tells her.

Roczi then turns around and walks out of the doctors office. She begins opening the container as she walks through the hall. By the time she makes it into the waiting room she has a drive in her hand and begins reading it.

The mission targets and objectives are so great and unexpected Roczi pauses before the doorway out of the labs. For a second time, she is stunned. Her eyes widen as the information about the mission continues to reveal itself.

"I have to get off this ship and stop this," Roczi thinks to herself.

Roczi quickly exits the door and is startled to see Desmond in the corridor waiting for her.

"So, those mission objectives set the bar pretty high. Are you excited to start?" Desmond asks.

Roczi's replies quickly, by drawing a magnetic pistol out from behind her back and putting four rounds through his main processors. Two are sent through his head and two more through his chest. She then scans for witnesses, but luckily there are none. Roczi quickly locates a nearby wall panel and drags Desmond's body to it. She opens the panel and picks up the nonfunctional machine.

"Sorry Desmond, but whatever your mission was I couldn't let you complete it," She says as she stuffs the body into the wall.

Roczi closes the panel and begins quickly walking down the hallway to the lower hanger bays. She needs to find a way back to Sam, and she's hoping to get it done before Desmond is declared missing, or his body is discovered. The bay where the November first docked and they initially met Suphran is her best bet. Roczi knows Sam will never forget the first time he boarded an alien spacecraft, so it makes the most logical extraction point.

Breaking an Entering

The smallest thread of metal, only recently malformed through a treacherous but necessary act of violence, begins to take back it's designed form. The thread delicately nears another and lets a few electrons through. More tiny threads near and form less-broken circuits. With each poor circuit formed, more electrons pass. Then there is a faint spark. This small spark is enough to bring a machine back to life, but only enough to know that it is dying. The machine frantically begins trying to save itself. It sends code anywhere throughout it's circuits till it receives an unknown code back. It translates the code to an appendage that has moved. The dying machine sends a barrage of signals to the appendage. The mechanical arm flails till it knocks a wall panel open in massive luxury spacecraft over forty-four-thousand light years away from its home planet. The machine does not yet realize that this set of actions has just secured it's continued existence, or how it's existence will impact sentient life.

With the panel open, light enters the space within the walls and the machine sees an organic life form peer in, and then another. A few minutes later the machine is pulled out of the wall and into a brightly lit corridor.

"That is Desmond. I just gave him his orders. The other machine must have done this. Sound the alarm I'll notify the commander," The Mirancris geneticist Doctor Minger orders his subordinates.

Throughout the infinite a subtle alarm sounds with a soft female voice.   "Infiltrator onboard. Please report inordinate behavior," The alarm repeats.

"What a pleasant call to arms...," Roczi thinks to herself as she makes her way to her target hanger.

Hearing the alarm as she nears the docking bay Roczi speeds up her pace, and grabs her communicator.

"Sam! My covers blown and I need extraction!" Roczi exclaims as she slowly changes back into her preferred form.

Sam is startled out of his nap, but quickly reacts. He answers his communicator in a confused manor.

"Already! Can I get a location or nav point?" Sam asks.

"The bay we first boarded through."

"Try to find a way to open the doors, or just get out somehow."

Then Rizac gets on the communicator and offers some help.

"Sam, send me the location. I may be able to provide some exit options for Roczi."

"Get these doors open and get on the November," Sam tells Rizac.

"That's not how it works. I need to get to a control center. It will take some time. Get Rox then comeback for me."

"O.K. Riz. Watch yourself, and we will come back for you," Sam says as he tries to reassure Rizac.

"Go!" Rizac tells Sam as the doors open for the November's departure.

Sam fly's the November out of the Gate's End, then maps the exterior of the Infinite with a navigation point on the targeted bay. He then sends the information to Rizac, Cloaks the November and makes his way to Roczi as fast as he can without breaking cloak.

On the Infinite Kiten arrives outside the labs to observe what the scientists have found. What she finds is two lab scientists, Doctor Minger and two of the bio-modified soldiers standing around Desmond's lightly twitching body.

"Who made the discovery?" Kiten asks as she approaches.

"I found it," One of the scientists answers boastfully.

Kiten pauses and looks at the her disapprovingly. Mirancris bio-scientist have a tendency toward arrogance. It is tendency Kiten is not fond of.

"Please brief me," Kiten requests.

"I had just left the labs for the..."

"I need the summary of the find, not the details of your day," Kiten tells her in a condescending manner.

"I heard the panel open, I looked inside, I found the machine and made notifications."

"Who sounded the alarm?" Kiten asks the group.

Doctor Minger (now realizing his mistake) faces Kiten and begrudgingly answers.

"That would be me."

"What was your purpose in notifying our intruder that we are aware of their presence?" Kiten asks.

"You will have to excuse my lack of security. All of my training is based around building armies. Isn't it your job to find this person? You might want to get started," Minger tells Kiten.

Unamused by the doctors tone, Kiten dismisses the bio-modified soldiers and unlocks her four arms from one another. She grabs the doctor and other two scientists by their necks. Then with her thin pale limbs picks up the Mirancris scientists.

"Everyone here is replaceable doctor, and I do believe your mission is complete. You must remember, It serves to remember ones position, but it also serves to remember one's situation Doctor," Kiten advises.

Releasing the scientists, she stands high above them and locks her arms back into place.

"Luckily, I have just found more work for you and your scientists. Take the machine into your

lab. I want to see what we can find out from it,"
Kiten explains as she walks away.

Doctor Minger and the scientists are left
gasping for air in the corridor. After they catch
their breath Doctor Minger looks at the others.

"You heard the creature. Take it in the lab. I
know exactly what I want to do with it," Minger
tells his staff.

Walking down the corridor Kiten quickly gets
on her communicator.

"Nico, I need you in place now. It seems they
too are moving before expected."

"Understood. I'm en route and I will be in
place in moments."

"Great work Niko. I'll be in place for you
once I'm finished."

Still onboard the Gates End, but within the
cold, airless space between the hulls, Rizac makes
his way to his destination. Only stopping to
occasionally disable sensors he used to set up and
maintain. Then he finds his target and enters a
maintenance corridor. Once again, his complete
knowledge of the Gate's End has been essential.
Walking through the corridor he gets to the final

wall panel, and slowly and quietly begins to open
it.

Confident in his abilities, Rizac decided not
to tell Sam the control center he will use to open
the exit paths for Roczi's extraction has another
name. It is more commonly called The Helm. Located
on the bridge, it is on the other side of the final
wall panel.

Rizac readies his suppressed sub-machine gun
and two concussive flash grenades. He then kicks
open the panel and enters the bridge throwing
grenades to the other side of the room. Rizac pours
fire steadily at the Mirancris bridge officers. The
ill-prepared bridge officers are no match for
Rizac's merciless surprise attack. He quickly kills
three before the other officers notice, but then
the grenades go off stunning and disorientating the
remaining four as they are knocked to the ground.
Rizac's space suit protects him from the blasts as
he walks to the downed bridge officers and executes
them without remorse. In a mater of mere seconds,
Rizac has retaken the bridge.

He hen secures the bridge further by locking
all the ships doors and elevators, essentially
putting the entire Gate's End on lockdown. The
mercenaries and other crew members will soon
realize the ship has been taken, so it's only a
matter of time before they reach the bridge. To
make matters worse, Rizac also knows machines will

reach him first. Holding them off will be next to impossible, so he must work fast.

"Now that I'm finished with that, let's liberate my ship and bring the Divine Gate out of hiding. I should go ahead and get Roczi out of her predicament as well," Rizac says aloud, enjoying his work.

Rizac restores the the ship to it's prewar power levels, and the interior of the ship lights up, revealing some the Gate's End's former glory. The exterior of the of the ship also lights up, by way of windows and navigation lights.

Onboard the November Sam's sensors detect a huge energy signature from the Gate's End. He puts it on the screen and finds a substantial amount of light coming from behind the massive steel plating suspended around the ship.

"Rizac, this is Sam. There is a very noticeable change in the Gate's End's energy signature. Is there anything I should know?" Sam asks through his communicator.

"I have taken the bridge, and I am in control of the helm," Is his reply.

Shocked, Sam cannot immediately reply.

"Please repeat. Cause I can't believe what I just heard."

"I have taken the bridge, and I am in control of the helm. Give me some time to get the ship into position, and tell Roczi she has minutes to find a place to brace for impact."

"Impact? What is your plan?"

"I plan on opening up the Infinite. You will want to stay clear till then."

Sam looks at the screen, and through the openings between the steel plates he see's the bow of the ship turning up toward the Infinite.

"Roczi! You need to find a place to brace yourself for impact!" Sam tells her through the communicator.

"How much time do I have."

"My best guess, about a minute."

"Copy Sam. I'll brace myself in the bay"

"I'll be there for you once it's clear. Careful Rox."

Roczi soon arrives at the bay's entrance. She opens the docking bay when in front of her, out of the nothing she is surprised by the flash of exploding powder, and a tungsten and lead projectile ripping through the left side of her body. The shot knocks her back against the wall and rips off her arm. Nico uncloaks and walks through the door with his rifle, and a device slowly pulsating light on his right arm. He fires again. This time into her leg, disabling it.

"Don't bother with the com. You won't be able to reach anyone, but what I will allow you to do is watch Sam die, then die yourself," Nico tells the the very damaged Roczi as he kicks her gun away.

Roczi quickly adjusts her systems to operate with her barely functional body. During this process she regains her ability to speak.

"You expect me to ask why you're doing this, don't you, but I don't care. I'm more excited to find out what Sam will do to you after he see's me. I'm guessing he'll be torn apart. Thank you for making it happen," Roczi manages to tell Nico.

On the Infinite, many of the helmsmen have turned their attention away from their regular duties to focus on the search for the intruder. They are so distracted in fact, that they don't concern themselves with the sudden energy spike from the Gate's End. As the lights came on in the giant warship they thought it to be a security measure, but now the Gate's End turns to face them and no one notices.

On the bridge of the Gate's End with engines on full Rizac begins his charge directly into the Infinite. With the ships alarms sounding with requests to change course and notices of eminent impact, Rizac Decides he has heard enough.

"Gate's End, stifle! I'm trying to liberate you!" He tells the ships computers, with what can only be described as an insane tone from it's captains chair.

"Gate's End continue on course, all forward full engines."

The Gate's End charges toward the Infinite, unimpeded by her own safety systems and unnoticed by either crew. The ship gets dangerously close before Rizac takes further action.

"Disengage armor plating fields."

With a short series of flashes the warships giant armor plating is set free.

"Fields are disengaged," The ships computer informs Rizac.

"All stop! Full reverse! This is not a suicide mission Gate's End! Whoooah!" Rizac exclaims followed by a sinister laugh.

The giant ship comes to an abrupt stop throwing the the giant steel plates, and all of the

ships occupants, forward. Rizac is also thrown
forward from the the captains chair and onto the
helm. From his new position on the bridge, Rizac
looks at the main screen and sees the newly
released plates flying toward the Infinite

Outside of the the Gate's End Rizac's sudden
stop was noticed by more than just the ship
occupants. On the November's bridge Sam for the
first time sees the Gate's End how it was meant to
be seen, as the Divine Gate. It is a beautiful,
brightly lit vessel. A perfectly symmetrical ship
with dual half domes on the top and bottom. It's
larger front domes once house the privileged, but
it is still beautiful. The smaller domes in the
rear were for operation staff, and it is also
beautiful. The top and bottom of the ship are
connected with hundreds of columns, and it is
comparable in size to the Infinite. Rizac's former
home was clearly a luxurious one.

On the Infinite they notice Rizac's sudden
stop in a different way. First there was a strange
noticeable shift on the ship, This was caused by
the Gate's End's reverse engines. This causes a
helmsmen to return to his station and put the
anomaly on the screen, but it is already to late.
With no time for aversive maneuvers, he calls for
the impact alarm, but the giant steel plates slam
into the Infinite before they can sound.

The plates rip through the shielding and into
the hull. One of the plates hits the columns

underneath the forward dome, completely severing the Columns from the rest of the ship. Through-out the remaining columns all life support and power are cut off.

The impact knocks Nico far forward through the now zero gravity corridor. Roczi prepared for the impact by putting her working arm through the wall and bracing herself, and as Nico and his jamming device are left tumbling down the corridor Roczi manages to warn Sam.

"Sam, it's a set up. Sending the info now, but you need to get out of here. I have separate important intel you need to get back to Van Tellure."

"Go ahead and send the info, but I'm not leaving without you."

"You really need to get back Sam!"

Sam doesn't bother to reply. Seeing shuttles and escape pod's begin to leave the very damaged Infinite, Sam breaks cloak and quickly lands the November on the outside of one of the severed columns. This is where he hopes to find Roczi.

Sam checks his suit, weapons, and ship scanners. Once again Sam will knowingly walk into a trap, but this will be the first time he has done it without Roczi. Even though he finds no signs of life and no energy signatures, he knows Roczi is in

there somewhere. Sam engages his suit's cloak and
slowly walks off the November, and onto the outside
of the column. He brings a high powered compact
firearm to reduce his weapons signatures,
remembering the quite, stealthy warfare he had seen
on Nictwar. Then he begins slowly making his way to
the opening Rizac made for Roczi's rescue at the
top of the broken columns.

A Dark White Horse

Disappointed he couldn't engage the enemy right off the November, Sam now suspects Roczi may have been killed or damaged, and is possibly being used as bait. The thoughts running through his mind begin to anger Sam, but he knows he must stay focused. He takes a breath and a moment to clear his head, then continues his search.

Sam reaches the top of the column and peers over. The cut made by the giant plate was not clean. Broken pillars of different sizes, and torn metal walls lay before him. Sam enters the labyrinth slowly looking for the center elevator shafts. When he does reach them, Sam takes smoke grenades and begins throwing them down the shafts. As he throws one down the second tube he notices movement and what looks like a door opening. Sam thought the shafts would be the best place for an ambush, and apparently so did Nico. Sam quickly makes his way to the fourth tube and dives in. He uses a propulsion cylinder to expedite his move to the bay level.

Nico is back in the corridors after being drawn out by Sam's grenade scare. Frustrated that he gave away his position he decides to toss frag grenades into the elevator shafts himself, Hoping to make quick work of Sam then call for Kiten for extraction. Nico walks quickly from elevator door to elevator door throwing a grenade in each one. The conclusion from the frags can be felt shaking the column.

Nico opens the door to the fourth shaft, but as he throws the frag in Sam dives through the door tackling him. Nico fly's backward with Sam latched onto him through the dark zero-gravity corridor. Nico uses his extensive combat training to grab Sam, and throw him further down the hall. As Sam tumbles through the corridor Nico reaches for his gun. Sam does the same, but before either can fire Nico's grenade explodes, sending fragments in all directions. Small, jagged pieces of metal rip through Nico's back then exit out his abdomen. The tears in his suit self seal, but short vacuum pulls on his wounds and leaving him in tremendous pain. This causes Nico to release his weapon and apply pressure to the wounds. As Nico settles up against a wall his weapon simply floats down the corridor and out of his reach.

Sam approaches Nico and shoots the pulsating anti-com device, destroying his right arm in the process.

"Where is the machine!? What have you done with her!?" Sam angrily asks through the communicator.

There is no answer from Nico. Sam stays just out of physical range and points his firearm at Nico's head.

"Facilitating this information is the only way you will survive."

Sam gives him a moment to answer, but when he doesn't Sam knows he has to neutralize the threat before he can continue his search.

"Sam wait!" Roczi's voice is heard coming through the communicator.

"We need to take him with us. We need to take him back," She tells him.

"Why would we do that?"

Roczi floats into the same corridor. Pulling herself along with her one arm till she reaches Nico.

"Cause it's Lieutenant Nico, and whatever they've done to him can be vital intel. Not to mention we can possibly save him," Roczi tells Sam as she removes Nico's dark outer visor, revealing his genetically modified eyes.

"What has happened to you?" Sam asks.

But all Sam gets from Nico is a cold, emotionless stair.

Sam restrains Nico and brings him onboard the November. There he is placed in a medical stasis chamber against his will, but there is little fight left in the lieutenant. Sam then carries Roczi to his captains chair and sets her in it.

"Where's Rizac?" Roczi asks Sam.

"Still onboard the Gate's's End."

"With five-hundred of the galaxies finest mercenaries gunning for him," Roczi adds.

"Try to reach him on the com."

Roczi pushes her broken body out of her seat and Hobbles to the helm. There she uses the November's more powerful communicator for the task, and Sam leaves the bridge while Roczi tries to get ahold of Rizac. She continues to try and reach him till Sam returns, but there is no sign of him.

"What do you want to do Sam?"

"I want to get off this column."

On the bridge of the Gate's End Rizac quiets the alarms as they go off.

"Interior hull breaches through port and starboard," The ships computer alarms.

"Put up all fields throughout the front inner hull," Rizac commands as a counter measure.

On the bridge's main screen Rizac watches as the devastated Infinite sparks and it's lights flicker. He watches patiently for the inevitable. He begins to grin as the planets large grey, ice covered moon emerges on the screen, and his smile widens as they get closer, and closer. When finally the moons gravity grabs the Infinite and pulls it into her. The capitol ship slams into the surface. Sparks fly as the ship's broken columns hit the surface, till the the large domed portion collapses on impact. Explosions, followed by small brief fires are seen as the ships oxygen is burned. The crash only takes a few moments, but the ship will continue to burn and smolder for days.

"Please log that I single handedly destroyed The Mirancris Capitol ship Infinite," Rizac tells the ships computer as he watches the Infinite crash against the moon's surface.

"The Event has been recorded Captain Rizac."

Rizac initially questions what he just heard. He then smiles and laughs at his newly appointed role, but Rizac is happy to know he will die with a captains title.

"Thank you for the promotion Gate's End! What brings this on?" He asks the computer.

"There are no other readable sentient life signs onboard this vessel. You Captain Rizac are the only remaining option."

Rizac stops to think about what this means for a moment. He wonders why the A.I. Mercenaries would be killing off the ships occupants. Then he realizes.

"It's a mutiny! Give me a report. What's happening on my ship?"

"Machine energy signatures have killed ninety-nine-point-nine-eight percent of all sentient life on this vessel. The Machine energy signatures are now slowly converging on the bridge,"

Rizac knows that this group of mercenaries with a capitol ship would be a very dangerous prospect for anything in the galaxy.

"Why wasn't I told about this?" Rizac asks.

"The order to stifle was given by you during my attempt Captain."

Rizac momentarily pauses to put his palm on his face, realizing his mistake.

"Gate's End, when my life signs are faint, or longer you are to scuttle this ship into the gas giant."

"Understood Captain Rizac. Scuttle is inevitable. There is an exterior hull breach. A machine energy signature has breached the outer hull."

"Give me a visual," Rizac orders.

The ship launches a probe from the outer skin of the ship. The probe sends back images of the A.I. Coming forth onto the outer hull of the ship. It's a large skinless beast of a machine. It's matte black armor is hard to see but it's size and energy signature are unmistakeable.

"I would like a view of the entire ship," Rizac requests.

As the probe's camera pans out Rizac for the first time in years sees the Gate's End as it was meant to be. Although coated black, the majestic light pouring out of the vessel remind him of the personal paradise it once was, but can never be again.

"Now I can die in peace," he tells himself.

Then Rizac's eyes widen, and he walks closer to the main screen.

"Or maybe I can live in peace? How am I getting the signal from the probe when the coms are disabled?" Rizac asks the computer.

"The probe is using a short video signal utilizing radio and optical coding. The optical coding is not normally used for communication."

Rizac takes a second to think about what he just heard. He then decides not to just lay down and die without a fight.

"Would it be possible to send a nav point using that signal?"

"Yes, but the probe may then be compromised and at risk. Furthermore, the machine energy signatures on the outer hull could read the signal."

"Gate's End, In Five minutes send a nav point beacon to the bridges outer hull on the probes signal. In seven minutes scuttle this ship," Rizac directs the ships computers.

With a definite time of destruction set, Rizac works quickly to reach the outer hull. He runs back to the maintenance corridor and quickly accesses the airless inner hull. Having the ships schematics permanently imprinted genetically to his memory aids his escape, and helps the Captain to the outer hull with twenty-one seconds to spare.

Standing on the outer hull Rizac prepares to hold his position. He readies his weapon and watches the time. The five minutes elapse, and Rizac's mood changes. He knows he stands no chance against the coming machines, but he is ready for death. He has done all he can, and he is happy with his final actions and the events he has witnessed. The view of the orange gas giant, and the still smoldering remains of the Infinite make him smile as he loosely holds his submachine gun. This has always been Rizac's favorite part of the ship, and he can think of no other place he'd rather spend his last moments, but Rizac can't enjoy the view long.

As he turns around, he sees the matte black armored mercenary he was warned of. He immediately recognizes Rizac's weapon as a non-threat and holsters his large caliber fire arm. This Machine just wants the organics of the ship, and doesn't feel the need to waste munitions. Rizac fires his submachine gun at the beastly machine, but to no avail. Rizac's weapon has zero effect on the mercenary as he continues forward.

Rizac now contemplates his options, but neither are good. Jump into space and slowly freeze as his suit runs out of power, or let the machine kill him (hopefully quickly). When his weapon runs out of ammunition he throws it at the machine. Rizac then closes his eyes and waits for the machine to end his life.

With every centimeter machine nears, Rizac's death also nears, but without reason the machine stops and turns it's head to one side. All of the sudden the machine is tumbling head over heels in space. Then Sam appears out of nowhere with a high powered rifle. The mercenary reaches for his weapon as he drifts through space, but Sam is at the ready with his two meter long, triple barred, high velocity magnetic rifle. Sam fires first, and the high velocity tungsten projectile hits the target cleanly. The kinetic energy is more than the machine can bare. Sam's target is transformed into fragments and broken parts. Small pieces of the threat splash onto Sam and Rizac as the November uncloaks where the mercenary once stood.

Rizac runs to the November and up her ramp, then Sam quickly follows. The ramp closes and seals. Then Sam quickly removes his helmet, dropping it to the ground.

"Get us home Rox!" Sam tells her.

"No wait!" Rizac exclaims, "I have to see her go."

Roczi takes the November off the hull and slowly backs the November away. It's quiet

throughout the ship as the three witness the final
moments of the Gate's End, as well as Rizac's past
and purpose.

As ordered by Captain Rizac, the great ship
turns it's bow toward the gas giant and begins to
descend into it. As it nears, the planet's massive
gravity pulls the ship apart, and under a minute
the Gate's End is is no more.

For a moment the November is silent as Sam and
Roczi wait for Rizac to make the call. With his
eyes still fixed on the main screen, Rizac decides
he has seen enough.

"Let's go home Sam."

Sam then looks at Roczi, and gives her a
subtle nod.

Confirmation

Days later Sam finds himself walking the corridors of the Escape. Once again he admires Rizac's handy work and reflects on the past weeks substantial events. He is also a little upset and at a bit of a loss as to why he hasn't yet received payment from Suphran. Sam began developing ideas to retrieve payment from the Strategist when he received communications on the bridge, and although it wasn't Suphran calling with payment, Sam is always happy to hear from Zac Van Tellure.

"Good to hear from you Zac. What you got for me?"

"Just giving you updates on the intel you brought us, and on lieutenant Nico's condition as you requested."

"Great! Do we have any idea what happened to Nico?"

"Yes, yes we do actually. We had Mirancris doctors help us with his condition. We found a new life form throughout his nervous system, including his brain. It's described as something between bacteria and fungus. The specimen is clearly an

older species and not designed, but the doctors
found definite signs of gene manipulation. He will
make a full recovery, but his brain can never be
fully freed of the life form, and the doctors will
continue looking into options for his eyes. Knowing
Nico, he'll probably go mechanical, but he will
still be given a pension and medical discharge. We
can't have him in his current condition."

"Sad, but your loss could be my gain. I'm
expecting a large jump in demand for my services.
I'll need good people with me."

"I'm happy to hear that Sam. He's to good a
soldier to be mothballed just yet," Zac tells Sam
with a nod.

"The intel you brought us was very concerning.
We notified the embassies of all the targeted
leaders and dignitaries. Besides strengthening our
own security that's all we can do with it, and
we're keeping the equipment you brought us to
ourselves for now, but our labs are checking them
out for counter measures," Zac continued.

"I'm assuming once the UNSA fully understands
the equipment and develops counter measures your
labs will take full credit, and funding," Sam says
to Zac with a smirk.

"How did you know? You don't have moles in my
outfit Sam. Do you?" Zac says jokingly.

Roczi's voice then comes over Sam's communicator.

"Sam, we are receiving a hale," She tells him.

"Zac, I'm being called away, but please let's stay in touch."

"Of course. We'll have drinks soon."

The communicator is then closed and Sam opens the hale. He is delighted by what he finds. Suphran's luxury ship is on screen, and there is not a single weapon or shielding alert.

"Roczi, what do we have here?"

Now fully repaired, and one-hundred percent functional, Roczi fills him in.

"Well, it's very strange... Kiten ,Yes Suphran's assistant, is requesting to dock the Tyzon onboard the station with Suphran and two technicians. She says it's to deliver our payment."

"Well Rox, you may have forgotten due to your injuries, but getting paid is what we do here. If your not interested in your portion I'll be happy to relieve you of the burdens money brings," Sam tells her.

"And what about me?" Rizac asks.

"I am fully aware of all your options Riz. I would hate for you to leave my employment for a previously held position, but I also know that position is no longer available," Sam says with a smile, but both Rizac and Roczi let there jaws drop from the insensitive comment.

"Get armed, and stay sharp. Then let's answer the door," Sam tells his crew.

Rizac gives Kiten the docking instructions, while Sam and Roczi go to the bay to greet their guests (as gracious hosts should).

The Tyzon then docks within the Escapes internal docking bay. Kiten exits first with Suphran coming down the stair ramp just after. Following are two Theon technicians. Sam and Roczi are left a little surprised that the Mirancris are already utilizing Theon labor.

"Suphran, I was beginning to wonder," Sam tells him.

"Understandably. My apologies. I have been overwhelmed with work, but I have added appropriate interest to your payment," Suphran informs Sam.

"I just can't stay mad at you Suphran. You know what matters to me."

Sam's statement puzzles Suphran and Kiten, but more noticeably, it embarrasses Roczi.

"Sam, these Theon are here to install the new stair ramp to your ship."

"I'll take them," Roczi say's as she motions for them to follow her.

Suphran then motions for Kiten to go with.

"We have a little time while your new equipment is being installed, and I have some questions about the report," Suphran tells Sam.

"Having Kiten here brings up my own."

"I have answers for you as well."

Sam again leads Suphran into the conference room, where they once again sit and briefly discuss the stations decor. Sam's most recently added art works, starships and of course politics make up the majority of the conversation, but when the small talk is spent they finally get to it.

"Why don't I start. Your report seems complete, but I don't understand why I wasn't sent notifications immediately after confirmations were made," Suphran tells Sam, expecting an explanation.

"We were hoping for a visual confirmation. That's when all hell broke loose. We were not expecting A.I. mutiny, but the timing seems to indicate that once Kaens was reached he was likely

killed. Most likely, at the beginning of the
event."

"Five-hundred machines with two capitol ships
and thousands of other craft pirating our trade
lanes could cripple our economies, further
straining relations between all societies. Whatever
the extremists reasons, they made the right
decision scuttling their ships," Suphran tells Sam
with intentional insincerity.

"I'm just glad that mess seemed to clean
itself up. What was Kiten doing onboard?"

"She was my agent inside. The only one I could
trust, but when Kaens refused to give their
location to her I had to get you involved. I knew
your machine could use her abilities to map their
location. Something Kiten could not."

"And what about 4 Vesta, the initial loss of
the capitol ships, or the ambush on the lower decks
of the Infinite? Many Humans lost their lives to a
war we had nothing to do with, and I came very
close to losing a good friend. Suphran, I know all
about loose ends, and I know a setup when I see
one," Sam tells him with anger in his voice.

"My actions have made you very wealthy, and I
can't be blamed for Humanities predictability. You
know the answers. Why would you ask? Does it
satisfy some repressed, emotional part of the Human
brain? Besides, your mission with the UNSA wasn't

diplomatic, it was designed to steal secrets, our only bargaining chips. Your people have a saying, "The end justifies the means," so one could say my actions were very Human."

The conference room is now dead silent as Sam and Suphran's anger cripples their ability to speak civilly, so they just glare at each other in the quite room. The awkward silence is finally broken when Suphran receives a notification from Kiten.

"Kiten to Suphran, the instillation is complete and the transaction is confirmed," Kiten informs him.

"Thank you Kiten. I'm just taking care of some loose ends with Captain Stix. I'll see you on the Tyzon momentarily."

"Is there anything else we need to discuss?" Suphran asks Sam.

"No. I think we are done here. Let me walk you to your ship."

They do not speak a word to each other as they walk to the docking bay. Nothing is said or gestured till Suphran is walking up the stair ramp to his ship.

"I'll see you again Sam."

"Yes. Yes you will."

Roczi picks up on Sam's elevated blood pressure and signs of stress, and as the two leave the bay and approach the bridge as Suphran's luxury ship departs for the second time. Soon Sam and Roczi enter the bridge and Rizac informs them that the Tyzon is no longer in sensory range. That is when Roczi decides to ask.

"What happened Sam? What got you so upset?"

"Suphran is a threat and a monster... So, nothing we didn't already know, but I did come to a decision."

"And what decision is that Sam?"

"I'm going to kill him."

www.ingramcontent.com/pod-product-compliance
Lightning Source LLC
Chambersburg PA
CBHW062016170626
46813CB00001B/180